Praise for *Sanguine and Stygian*

"It's hard to even put how much I love this book into words. It's intense, steamy, and had such a great dark fantasy vibe."

-Amazon Reviewer

"Hands down one of the best fantasy romances out there."

-CJ Connor

"This book grips you from the beginning and doesn't let go. From the opening scene to the last sentence, you are wanting more. You just have to find out what happens next, and suddenly it's 2AM and you have to get up for work in 4 hours! Action, intrigue, magic, and romance!"

-Amazon Reviewer

"From the first page, you dive into this amazing fantasy realm full of magic & mercenaries. Fast paced with great characters and steamy romance scenes, you won't be able to put this book down.

-Bridget K. Shapiro

"Good luck sleeping! You won't want to put this one down. Action packed and full of heat and intrigue, you'll love the merry band of bawdy characters from start to finish... this book will whet your appetite for much more."

-Amazon Reviewer

ALSO BY SARA SELLERS

Sanguine and Stygian

The Stygian Crown

THE STORM KING

SARA SELLERS

Paperback ISBN: 978-1-7372194-5-3

Cover Design by Ravven
www.ravven.com

www.sarasellers.com

To lucky number three.

CHAPTER I
VALLA

Valla hated winter. She burrowed deeper into her cloak, wrapping her arms around herself and shoving her hands into her armpits. A bone deep chill had begun seeping through her blood as soon as they crossed into her betrothed's territory. Now, trudging through knee-deep snow on his accursed mountain, she was riddled with it. Frost coated her eyelashes. An intimate, unrelenting cold—the kind of cold she'd never known before—rattled her teeth and shook her in her sleep.

She was summer's child. The sun princess. Her life to this point had been summer's hot kiss and long shadows. Heated lakes and the patter of feet on blistering sandstone before a rainfall.

"How much farther?" Valla asked. She hunched over the fire struggling to stay lit against the blinding snowfall. The entourage escorting Valla to her future husband had not come prepared for winter's persistent wrath. They'd lost one of the horses to a hidden gully beneath the snow three days ago, and it'd been slow-going since then. Their clothes weren't suited to the cold damp, and their tents had blown to pieces in the harsh wind.

"A day or two at most," Stefan said, fingers close enough to the fire for the flames to lick at his skin. He was her father's fire mage and Valla's appointed keeper for this trip, present to ensure she didn't lose her way on her journey into the enemy's arms. Stefan and three of her father's radiant guard made up their retinue. But Stefan's powers were useless without the sun to power them, and this high on the mountain, snow clouds blocked out the sun.

"I might die by then."

Snow fell on the mountain like rain, torrential and unrelenting. Valla thought she may never feel warm again. She'd all but forgotten what the caress of the sun's rays felt like. She peered through the blizzard toward their destination. The Storm King's hall glowed, a bright beacon atop the mountain. The mountain was known to her betrothed's people as Jotunfjall. To ascend it was a test in and of itself. Only the strong could make it there, were offered its sustenance. It was an instrument of his unbending will.

They were forced to keep moving or be buried beneath snowfall, and Valla stared back longingly at the choking flames as they trudged ahead. It was a fitting metaphor for her current predicament. After all, what could Rodrick Fjallgard, king of winter, offer her of summer's embrace in this barren wasteland? She feared she would be snuffed out, a fading flame caged in cold, endless night.

Their party neared a bend in the mountain where the thin path narrowed treacherously. Valla clung to rocky outcrops as she skirted her way along the steep edge, forcing herself not to look down.

Stefan shook off the snow piling atop his wide-brimmed hat and sighed. "Don't know what I did to be assigned this mission."

"You're welcome to leave at any time," Valla said. Her father's favored fire mage was no friend of hers. When she'd first begun her monthly courses, he'd been the one to brand the Sun King's symbol into her hip with a spell.

Her father's daughters got no better treatment than his livestock. A stamp of her worth, of her breedable belly ready for the most advantageous trade he could muster. The magic had been no anesthetic, either. A metal brand heated by fire would have served just as well.

"You keep saying that, darling, I might just take you up on it."

The party inched their way forward single file, leading the horses rather than risk riding. Valla and Stefan brought up the rear. A sound like distant thunder echoed across the mountain range, muted by the ripping wind. Small trails of snow settled atop Jotunfjall's jagged edges jumped and shuddered. The guards began to whisper amongst themselves.

"What is that noise?" Valla asked.

A fresh pelt of snow hit her, and she blinked up through the sheet of snowfall. A cloud of white floating near the mountain's peak ballooned outward, gaining mass.

"What is that?" Her voice rose in pitch as the mass of snow grew larger. Was it moving toward them?

"Spirits," a guard said.

"Turn around!" someone snapped. "We have to reach cover before that thing reaches us."

"An avalanche," Stefan said, staring unblinking at the sky. "It will bury us."

Valla turned, heart racing in her chest, and began scrambling back down the trail. But it was impossible to run in snow this deep, and their party was slow and clumped.

The rumble grew closer. Stefan's hands shoved at her back, urging her to go faster, nearly making her lose her balance.

"Move, bitch," one of the guards yelled, and he thundered

past them on a horse. The other guards followed, and Valla clung to the side of the mountain with stiff fingers.

The roaring surrounded them. Wind whipped past her ears. The third guard slipped as he scrambled past her and Stefan. His body careened towards the path's perilous edge.

"No!" Valla shouted as he disappeared, taking a chunk of snow with him.

His scream lasted a small eternity.

"Go, Valla!" Stefan yelled.

Then weight slammed into her back, and she was falling forward, tumbling face-first into the snow. Her head slammed into something hard. Stars exploded in her vision. Blackness descended like a thick blanket, and Valla was warm at last.

CHAPTER 2
VALLA

Valla woke to darkness and ice and pain. Her skull throbbed. Cold surrounded her, soaked through her. She sucked a reedy breath into straining lungs. She clawed blindly, ice and rocks jamming deep beneath her nails as she shoved snow out of the way.

She would not be buried on this mountain. She would not give her future husband the pleasure of her timely demise. But how did she know if she was digging in the right direction?

Valla renewed her effort with a frenzy. Panic squeezed her throat and seared her lungs. Her hand broke through snow to biting wind, and she surged forward, gasping as she broke free.

She collapsed on her back and drew in deep breaths. Snowflakes prickled her eyes.

The cold returned with a vengeance, digging through her sodden clothes and hair. Darkness had fallen, and only the stars and the distant glow of the Storm King's fortress aided her vision. Pale snow as far as the eye could see, and that jagged rock piercing the sky. No guards. No Stefan. No horses. And worst of all, no fire or food. The horses had been carrying their supplies.

Valla's chest tightened, and she forced herself to take slow breaths. She was the Sun King's daughter. She could do this. This mountain was nothing compared to the oppressive heat of a southern summer, the relentless beat of the sun on raw skin, or the deadly monsoons that plagued their coast. She'd weathered sunburns worse than this. But skin grew back. Toes didn't.

There was only forward—going back down the mountain was a death sentence. She had to reach the Storm King's fortress before cold, darkness, and hunger took her. Valla began to crawl.

Rodrick

RODRICK SHRUGGED on his white icebear fur and avoided his face in the mirror. He shouldn't be worried what his southern bride might think of him, but he hadn't managed to suppress every vain impulse of his youth quite yet.

He was not handsome in the traditional sense—especially compared to the smooth golden skin and dark, lustrous hair his wife would be accustomed to. His skin was weathered by winter, his blond hair already streaking through with strands of grey despite his thirty years of age. A jagged scar slashed through his eyebrow, courtesy of the icebear whose fur he now wore. He was lucky he'd kept the eye.

"Never thought I'd see you married," Astrid said. She'd been his friend since childhood and had grown into one of his finest warriors.

"It's for Frostheim."

"You condemn yourself to a lifetime of unhappiness."

Rodrick shook his head. "I'd rather suffer for my people than the other way around."

Astrid rolled her eyes. "Such a martyr. You wanna see what she looks like, at least? *His Brightness* Radagon sent a portrait."

"I'd rather not know my doom as it marches toward me."

"And to think I found you unbearable before."

Astrid set the Sun King's letter on his desk. "Suit yourself. You ready to face the council?"

"If I must. But the deal is done, the treaty signed. They won't sway me."

Rodrick followed Astrid to the council chamber, where three elders sat around a stone table. He took his seat and rolled his shoulders, while Astrid took up her place by the door.

Grey Torvald cleared his throat with a phlegmy cough. "King Rodrick, if you really intend to go through with this, we need to have a plan in place before your bride arrives. The frost heart's always been passed to children born of two Frostheim natives. There's no way to be sure the Isaanan princess can produce a suitable heir."

"Only an heir of winter can sit the winter throne," Elder Ulf said, steepling his gnarled fingers.

"You have no heirs, no siblings, no cousins. You've been warring with Isaana with little regard for your personal safety. If you die without a successor, what will we do? It will be chaos," Ymir said.

Rodrick sucked in cold air through his nostrils. The frost heart was the name of the magic passed through his family line for the past three hundred years. It was a valuable source of power for warring and managing Jotunfjall's dangerous weather, but it came at a steep price. The bearer of the frost heart couldn't be away from Frostheim for too long without growing ill and eventually dying. It'd been a complicating factor in his southern campaigns, and he was relieved the Isaanans were coming to him, for once.

"And what do you propose I do? Without a Sunstar in my bed, we do not eat. Is that what you wish?"

"The frost heart is worth thousands of lives," Elder Ulf said.

Rodrick's jaw ticked, and he struggled to hold his tongue.

"You should take a mistress," Grey Torvald said. "Sire a child with her first, and name them as your heir before you risk impregnating the Sunstar. The line of inheritance must be uncontested."

"And do you plan to supervise our bedroom activities to ensure I don't pump her full of magic seed?"

Astrid snorted. Torvald's face wrinkled even further, his lips pinching together. "You are a young king yet. This is a serious matter."

Rodrick pushed up from the table, ice pricking at his fingertips. "I'll hear no more of this. The frost seed is as much curse as it is boon, and I won't let it dictate my life any further than it already has."

"But sire—" Ymir started.

"Enough!" Rodrick slammed a hand down on the table, and a sheet of dark ice sliced across the stone, splintering into a thousand tiny cracks. The elders pulled back in their chairs.

"You insult me and your future *Queen* to my face because of unfounded supposition. You talk of breeding and bloodlines and traits like I'm your prized stallion. I'm your king, not your puppet, and I will be treated as such. As will my wife."

Rodrick strode out of the room, slamming the door behind him.

RODRICK RESISTED OPENING the Sun King's letter for the rest of the day, until curiosity and lingering unease from the council meeting got the better of him. The top sheet was a stamped and signed copy of the terms and conditions of Frostheim's truce with Isaana. A cease to their warring in exchange for opening trade and giving his people access to fertile land at the base of the mountain, so they might better sustain themselves. And Radagon Sunstar's oldest daughter's hand in marriage, to seal the deal.

Rodrick flipped to the next page, where his intended's likeness had been sketched in charcoal by a master. They'd sent her portrait to sweeten the deal, but Rodrick hadn't needed to look at it. He would've married her regardless, for the good of his people. And as his own grizzled visage attested, looks faded. Especially in a clime as harsh as his.

His intended was beautiful, but he'd expected as much. Why else send a portrait? She had a petite, heart-shaped face clouded by dark curls that begged for the clench of a man's fist. Dark eyes and thick lashes, a stubborn tilt to her jaw. Her eyes flashed fire at the artist, daring them to capture her as anything other than what she was.

Rodrick folded up the letter and shoved it into his desk drawer. She would do.

CHAPTER 3
VALLA

Valla followed the light of the Storm King's hall like a guiding star. She moved slowly but efficiently, keeping close to the side of the mountain and testing for gullies hidden in the snow with a broken stick she'd found. She had a renewed sense of purpose—something to focus on other than the unrelenting cold and her impending nuptials.

Survival.

She saw no signs of Stefan or her guards. Nothing disturbed the even snow except the deep imprints of her footsteps. The mountain was quiet but for the howl of the wind and the distant yowling of the snowcats.

Time surely passed, but she had a poor sense of it in this frozen environment. The only thing that changed was the distant light growing closer with each ragged step.

Instead, she measured time by the failings of her body. First, wind had chapped every inch of her exposed skin. Then her fingers had stiffened, and she struggled to grip her stick. Now, her entire body ached, from her heavy eyelids to the base of her spine and the arches of her feet. But she couldn't stop, couldn't sleep. She might be lulled into the warmth of oblivion and never wake back up.

Valla occupied her mind by raging at her future husband. What kind of person would *choose* to live up here? This frozen icicle on the tip of the world. No wonder they warred with Isaana so much; home was an icy hellhole. She would do him the disservice of surviving, and she would make him regret ever bringing her to this wretched place.

When her sunken belly began to growl with hunger, to quiet her appetite she imagined biting into a ball of packed ice and pain shooting through her sensitive teeth. She bet they actually ate ice here. Probably flavored with the lifeblood of some poor animal. Penguin blood snowbowls. Valla snorted and took another step.

WHEN THE FORTRESS gates came into sight in the distance, Valla tried to yell for help. Her voice came out in a croaky rasp. She waded through the snow towards the flickering lights, her vision hazy. Two dark blobs on the horizon morphed into two guards standing at the gates, layered so deep in furs she could barely see their faces. They each had a small brazier of coals beside them that glowed red with warmth.

Valla scurried forward and collapsed in front of a brazier, holding her hands and face over the coals. Her icy skin stung from the sudden heat. She wanted to shovel the coals into her mouth and swallow them down—to eat their warmth and make it her own.

One of the guards lowered a spear to her throat, nudging the sharp tip inside her cloak. Valla glared up at him.

"Who are you, she-beast? What are you doing on Jotunfjall?"

Valla cackled hysterically, her throat ripped and raw. A woman appeared out of the darkness alone, poorly dressed and blue from cold—with no supplies to speak of—and they greeted her like this? Were all Frostheimers such brutes?

"I'm from the south. Please, I need help, food—"

The guards looked to each other, then nodded at the gates. "Go. You must introduce yourself to the Fjallgard. He will decide if you're worthy to stay."

Valla stumbled to her feet, tearing herself away from the brazier's warmth by force of will alone. Icicles clung to the high, twisted gates that led to the fortress. Spikes at the bottom drove deep into the snow, securing the doors. What use were gates, atop the tallest fucking mountain in Valenmur? Did her betrothed fear a siege?

Valla slid through the small gap in the iron doors.

The Storm King's fortress was unassuming compared to the Sun Palace, but then, so was a peacock. Built of solid timber and stone, it was as unwelcoming as its surroundings. There were few windows to let the sun in, but she supposed that kept it well insulated.

From the sounds within the fortress, there was a celebration going on. She was already imagining the roaring fire and hot meal awaiting her. A great flickering light drew her eye upward. A side path studded with torches wound up to the very peak of the mountain—and at the top, a giant bowl of fire rippled in the wind. Her beacon. Her saving grace.

Valla took a stabilizing breath as she pulled open the tall, creaking door to the keep, sobering to the reality awaiting within. There was no going back down the mountain. This was it. She'd make the best of it, just as she always had.

She entered a great hall packed to the rafters. The chaos of noise, movement, and scents after weeks of icy wasteland threatened to overwhelm her. People were singing, dancing, drinking, arm-wrestling. Long tables lined the hall, teeming with food and people.

Valla grimaced. One of the Storm King's main reasons for

warring with her father was the lack of crops that could be grown in this accursed place, but their larders must be fat from the autumn raids.

The largest fireplace she'd ever seen took up the far wall. Five people could stand abreast inside it with room to spare. She made a beeline for it, keeping her head low and ignoring the curious glances of the revelers. She stood out as a foreigner amongst these tall, pale creatures with piercing blue eyes. They had broad northern frames and wore layers of fur and leather. She fit the southern archetype—burnished skin, dark hair, and a short, curvy frame.

Valla squeezed through two giant men drinking beer from tankards the size of her head, then threw herself to her knees in front of the fireplace. She began stripping off her sodden outer layers, even her boots and socks. There should have been more clothing to remove, but she'd been ill-prepared for this journey from the start. Almost as if her father hadn't wanted them to make it.

Valla thrust her hands toward the flame and rubbed them together. Her eyes closed as heat sunk into her. Delicious warm energy began to crawl back into her hands and feet. It was no summer sun, but it would do. She stretched her toes, burying them into the fur rug beneath her. A mouthwatering smell filled the hall. Roasting meat and sizzling onions. Her stomach growled.

Valla sat back on her heels, still as close to the roaring fire as she could stand, until the ends of her hair began to dry and her teeth stopped chattering. She almost felt human again. Eventually the nearness of the flames began to burn her eyes. The bone deep ache and sore muscles from her trek through the snow were making themselves known as her adrenaline waned.

An enormous chair with wide, rounded arms and a padded seat sat just out of reach of the fire, and it was piled with thick white furs. Odd, that no one had claimed it when the hall was so full, but their loss was her gain. It was high enough that when she sat, her bare feet dangled several inches above the floor. Valla curled her legs beneath her and drug one of the furs up to her chin. It was pure white, deliciously soft, and already toasty from the fire. She sighed in contentment. All she needed now was a full belly.

"I didn't know we were gonna get a show," one of the men by the hearth said.

"Should we tell her?" asked the other.

Valla ignored them and closed her eyes. The crackle of the fire soothed her frayed nerves. Bundled up like this, it was a matter of minutes before she'd be fast asleep.

The din of the party fell away as a large shadow fell over her, blocking the heat of the fire. *Sunmother, couldn't they see she was resting?*

The party fell silent, and Valla blinked. Hundreds of icy blue eyes stared at her in shock, but one pair burned brighter than all the rest, glowering at her from overhead. Her silver-eyed shadow.

The man blocking the fire was taller than the average northman—which was saying something—and he had a wicked scar cutting through his left eyebrow. His face and body looked like they'd been hewn from the mountain itself. He wasn't particularly ugly or handsome, but intense, rugged. Utterly intimidating. He was less pale than many of the others, as if he'd spent some time in the Isaanan sun. Greys frosted his shoulder-length dirty blond hair, giving him a distinguished look. A bulky white fur was draped across his broad shoulders. It matched the one she was currently swaddled in.

"You're blocking the fire," she said.

The man looked up at the wooden beams on the ceiling and let out a dark laugh. Valla admired the flex and bob of his corded throat. A few uneasy chuckles filtered out of the onlookers, but the majority remained silent.

He looked back down at her, curiosity flickering over his hard face.

"You're in my seat." His voice was cutting, but a hint of mirth played at the edges of his eyes.

"No one was sitting here."

"Nevertheless, it is mine."

Valla sighed and pouted. "Must I give it up?"

The man's lips tightened and twisted like he was trying to hold in a laugh. "I'm afraid so."

Valla grunted and slid her legs out from under her. She'd been *this* close to falling asleep. She draped the fur around her, hopped to the ground, and stepped away, offering him the chair with a bow and a flourish.

A chorus of breaths being sucked in at once swelled throughout the room. Valla looked up.

The formerly pristine white furs still draped over the chair were streaked with dark mud from her dirty body.

Valla swallowed thickly and looked up at the man. His eyes were narrowed on the chair, a tight frown on his face. The space between his eyebrows tightened into a wrinkle. The two men by the hearth wore stark fear on their faces.

"I can clean it."

She couldn't. She had no idea where to begin, how to go about it without ruining the fur—she'd never washed a single thing in her life, much to her consternation now, but everyone seemed quite upset about the furs. The most cleaning she'd ever done was helping the servants dust the books in the palace library when she was bored out of her skull, which usually ended with an abandoned feather duster and her curled up in a chair with a new discovery.

The man lowered his big body into the chair, mud and all. He filled it out properly; she must have looked like a child sitting in it. He propped an elbow on the chair arm and leaned his head into his hand.

"Southerners do not often visit my court, but when they do, I expect them to properly introduce themselves."

Valla froze, her body stiffening. Her brain was still snow-fogged. *My court. His* court.

Her eyes swung about the room. Everyone watched the scene she'd grown an unfortunate role in. The chair had been empty because they'd known whose chair it was. Whose furs she'd muddied and still had wrapped around herself. She shot daggers at the two men by the hearth. They'd known all along.

Valla gulped as she turned back to her betrothed. Sitting in his chair, throne or not, he looked every inch a king. "You're the Storm King?" *Rodrick Fjallgard*. Her future husband.

He tilted his head. Lightning crackled behind his eyes, the air grew heavy with potential, and all the hair on her body stood on end as primordial fear snaked down her spine. It thrilled her, even as she fought the urge to run.

Valla lowered herself to her knees in front of him and bowed her head until it was even with his fur-wrapped boots. It rankled her to give him such deference, but she was reliant on his goodwill now. She knew nobles who would execute someone for what she'd just done. Had her father sent a picture of her likeness to the Storm King prior to their betrothal? Would he recognize her?

"Forgive me, your highness. I was much overcome by the cold when I arrived."

"You must have suffered if you came to my mountain dressed like that."

Valla nodded. "An oversight I've much lamented. Now I seek shelter, my lord."

"From?" His voice was warmth and smoke.

"Winter."

Rodrick chuckled. "Good luck hiding from her."

Valla swallowed her spit. The dirty fur had given her an idea—a stupid, reckless idea, but she'd survived the impossible already. She had little left to lose besides her freedom.

"Sunmother forgive me, I bear unfortunate news. I was part of Princess Seraphina's party that set out from Sunstone —her lady's maid. We were overcome by an avalanche a few days past. I woke buried in snow, with no sign of the others around. I had to make my way here for any chance at survival."

Rodrick's eyebrows shot up. A ripple of uneasy murmurs rose around them.

He gestured to a man on his right. "Send out a search party. Take light and shovels and the dogs." Then he focused that icy gaze of his on her again and narrowed his eyebrows. "And what of the princess?"

Valla shook her head and let her lip quiver. "I fear she may be lost to us, your highness. I barely survived myself. I was lucky, but my lady was at the head of the procession—the first to go under the snow. I searched for her, my lord, but it was so dark and cold. I feared for my life."

Rodrick stared at her intently, scanning her face until he appeared to make up his mind about something. Then his mouth twisted into a grimace. "Piss poor time to climb Jotunfjall's back. Not sure what your fool king was thinking, sending his daughter into a blizzard. I offered an escort of northmen months ago. Insisted, even, but was rebuked."

That did sound like her father. Always prideful to a fault. Her guardsmen would be alive, could return to their families right now if her father had taken the Storm King up on his offer. She had no love lost for Stefan, but suffocating in the snow was no way to go for a fire mage.

But their loss could give her a new lease on life—an opportunity to deceive the King of Frostheim and escape instead of being shackled to the brute forever, forced to whelp his babes and slowly freeze to death atop this rock.

"It was an arduous journey. We were ill prepared."

"It shouldn't surprise me that the Sun King would throw his own daughter to the storms to get my boot off his neck. How many daughters does he have, again?"

Valla bit her cheek. "Three."

Rodrick smirked. "So many? Perhaps he'll send me another. The eldest must have curried his disfavor to win the prize of marrying me. Tell me, was she the amenable sort?"

Valla's eyes flashed up at him, then she forced herself to look back down at his boots. "As amenable as one might expect, my lord. Given the circumstances." If she'd had doubts about the wisdom of deceiving him, they were fast fading in light of his arrogance.

"You did well to survive. Perhaps you have a bit of winter in you. But if your princess is indeed dead, what shall you do at my court? Our larder is light, and we've many mouths to feed this winter."

"I will leave at the earliest opportunity. Allow me to write to—"

He waved his hand in dismissal. "You will not be able to return to the capital until spring. The climb was treacherous when you made it. Now it is deadly. The rocks will begin to ice. Night will black out the sun. Jorumungar's Pass will be buried in snow till spring thaw. But all here earn their keep, especially when winter is nigh."

"*What?*" Hope trickled from her breast. He was joking, right? She couldn't stay here until spring. Winter had only just begun, and in the north it lasted for months! She wasn't surprised he wanted to put her to work, but she had few skills she imagined he'd find useful. She'd had servants for everything at the Sun Palace. Which meant the longer she was stuck on this sunforsaken mountain, the more likely her ruse would be discovered. And then there'd be hell to pay.

"As your princess learned, it's a death sentence to navigate the pass this late in the year."

Fuck. She could handle hair and dresses, at least. "Perhaps a lady in your court needs a maid—"

A small shake of his head. "We don't have such frippery here."

Valla floundered. "I'm educated. I could serve as a governess or tutor, perhaps? You must have children here."

"You're Isaanan. What could you teach them?"

Valla chewed her lip. She knew precious little about Frostheim, and she was beginning to wish she'd paid more attention to her own tutor's history lessons, as biased as they may have been.

Rodrick slowly shook his head. "No Frostheimer is going to let an Isaanan maid teach their children. My head hearthkeeper is always in search of young backs. I will let her place you where she needs."

Valla inclined her head. "As you wish." As long as he wasn't tossing her out into the snow, she could make do. She was the Storm King's bride. A summer princess banished from the sun. A prize offered up in a desperate bid for peace. And now, a servant to the enemy.

Rodrick smiled. "Then it's settled. You may freely partake of my feast, and Hearthkeeper Frieda will show you to your sleeping chambers this evening. Have you a name, lady's maid?"

"Valla." It was a name only her sisters called her, and thus shouldn't raise suspicion. To all else she was Lady Seraphina Sunstar of Isaana.

"Welcome to Frostheim, Valla."

Valla stood on shaky knees and began scanning the room for a flagon of alcohol. A cask of wine sat atop one of the long stone tables nearby.

"Valla?"

The Storm King's voice curled around her, and she glanced back at him. "Yes?"

"My fur?"

Valla reluctantly slid it off and passed it to him.

"Ah, I see you've managed to keep this one clean."

Valla flushed and marched off towards the wine, bare feet freezing against the stone floor, but she was intercepted before she got there. A woman with long blonde hair plaited into several braids bounded up to her and thrust a warm ceramic mug into her hands. The woman towered over her; Valla's head only came up to her breasts.

"Drink. You'll feel better. You look like an ice wraith curled up in your bed."

"Are you Frieda?"

"Frost no. I'm Astrid."

Valla took a big gulp from the mug and sputtered as fire raced down her throat. It was liquor mixed with something—but mostly liquor. It tasted awful, but the heat quickly traveled from her throat to her stomach, and tendrils of warmth unfurled inside her.

Astrid smiled. "Dragon's milk. Flame like no other. Some say if you drink enough of it, you'll belch fire. Gets you too drunk to remember if you succeeded in the morning, though."

Valla grinned and spread both hands around the warm mug, but her fingers still didn't touch. Were all the cups in the north so large? "Thank you. It's not from an actual dragon, is it?"

Astrid snorted. "You don't know much about Frostheim, do you?"

"I've spent my entire life in Sunstone. Isaana's capital," she added for clarification.

Astrid's eyes hardened a bit. "More's the pity. No, no winged ice lizards here, just as you've no flamin' beasts in the south anymore. It's mixed with goat's milk, truth be told, but those beasts are ornery and horned enough to have won the moniker." She tipped her head towards the hearth. "I take it he's assigned you to Frieda?"

Valla nodded.

"Drink up, then. You're gonna need it to deal with that frigid bat. Let me know if she's treating you poorly. We don't oft get visitors on the mountain, don't need the likes of her running 'em off."

Valla took a smaller sip this time, and it went down easier. "He's nothing like I'd imagined."

"Who? Rodrick?"

"The Storm King."

"He hates being called that, though he'll never admit it."

"I can sympathize."

Astrid's brows lifted. "Can you?"

Valla's eyes flitted over to the fire. Rodrick sat on his makeshift throne, crackling gaze staring into the flames. His long legs were sprawled wide. A giant white dog had joined him and lay at their master's feet in a cloud of fur.

Her intended was younger than Valla had pictured, though he wore the stresses of leadership in the crow's feet crinkling the corners of his eyes and the dark shadows beneath. A short golden beard lined his chin, softening his harsh face. The hall was full of men with beards of all shapes and sizes— some braided and beaded as ornately as the women's hair. Valla was unused to seeing facial hair on men, but she found she liked it. The Frostheimers weren't so particular about being clean-shaven as her Isaanan brethren, who would sooner melt away than weather the summer heat with a hair more than necessary.

Astrid tutted beneath her breath. "I've seen that look before."

Valla tore her eyes away from Rodrick. "I'm sorry, I just... Things are very different here. Is that his throne?"

Astrid snorted. "No, we've a clunky monstrosity we drag out for scaring foreign dignitaries, but it is the best seat in the hall. So, what news of the world below? And are you sure you weren't flown here by some great tropical bird? No one makes it through the pass after winter's first kiss, especially a southerner."

"Is that how you'd describe a blizzard and an avalanche? A *kiss*?"

Astrid smirked.

CHAPTER 4
RODRICK

Rodrick frowned as his intended sat cross-legged on the dining table bench and spoke with Astrid. As if she belonged here. As if he'd let her relax. She lied to his face with such ease—a talent she must have inherited from her traitorous father.

It was a pity his betrothed was so beautiful, as they would never make it to the altar at this rate. She was tiny, tan, and curved in all the right places, with big brown eyes that begged you to give her the world. But her skin sat tight on her face like she hadn't had much food or water in several days, and her cheeks were ruddy and chapped from windblast. She swayed back and forth, head nodding forward as she struggled to stay awake.

To anyone who'd spent any time in Isaana, her status was obvious. She had the easy, relaxed way of being of the southern nobles. Their posture was terrible—they spent all day lounging and enjoying the fruits of their bountiful harvests and the labor of their lessers. And when their people suffered war or nature's wrath, they languished in the Sun Palace, apart from it all.

Despite that, there was an undercurrent of steel in her gaze when she met his eyes. Perhaps she had more backbone than Radagon. That would be refreshing. Something to entertain himself with until the spring thaw came, and war returned to Valenmur.

The girl must not want to marry him, if she was willing to go to such lengths to avoid it. And truce or no, Rodrick wouldn't force his cock or his cursed seed on her. He knew too well what it was like to not have a choice. There were other routes to dealing with Isaana, albeit bloodier.

Rodrick had struggled to keep from laughing when she'd claimed to be a lady's maid. Her, with her butter soft skin and the gaze of a queen. At least she wasn't wholly her father's creature. She had her own dreams and wishes, and the mettle to seek them out.

He ought to offer her a bed for the night, let her rest up before subjecting her to Frieda. But he hadn't expected her bald lies, and his response had been harsh. He'd test that spine of hers as he taught her the true nature of the north. Rodrick was confident she'd confess soon and beg him to return her to her life of comforts. His hearthkeeper made grown men cry with regularity, so he looked forward to seeing what she could do with the pampered princess.

Across the room, Frieda marched Valla off to bed, and Astrid returned to his side.

"Odd, that one. Sure you don't wanna join the mission going down the mountain? Second party's heading out at dawn."

"Why should I? My princess is warm and sheltered, with a belly full of dragon's milk."

Astrid scrunched her face, then did a double take between him and the door Valla had left through. "What—"

"She lied. That's the Sunstar of Isaana you were chatting with."

Astrid stilled, then burst into a laugh. "Oh gods. And how long are you going to let this charade continue?"

"She'll confess soon enough. I've given her to Frieda, after all."

Astrid's lips twisted. "Frieda's father died in our last war with Isaana. Are you sure it's wise to put their crown jewel into her care?"

"I can think of no truer test of character."

"You're a cruel man, Rodrick Fjallgard."

"Search for the ones who accompanied her, but don't risk any lives trying to find them if the snows grow too heavy. We've got the one we want. The others can freeze."

"This could backfire, you know. Are you so eager to return to warring?"

"The king of summer sent his first daughter to her death. It makes me doubt his commitment to our truce."

"Still, she shouldn't have to suffer for his failings."

Rodrick shrugged. "If she wishes to go to such lengths to avoid marrying me, I'll not force the woman. She has sisters, does she not?"

"And if others discover who she is without the protection of being your wife? You know many still oppose this marriage."

"I'll be keeping a close eye on her. And so will you."

Astrid blew her bangs out of her face.

Rodrick bent down to scratch his tundra hound, Nanook, behind her ears. "What would you have me do?"

"Frieda will break her. But you don't break a feral snowcat. You tempt it, little by little, until it comes to you of its own volition."

Rodrick smirked. His bride *had* resembled a wet, feral cat. "I'll bear that in mind."

Rodrick returned to his office that evening and took the princess's portrait out of his desk, snapping it open. It was her, undoubtedly so. She was all the more enchanting in person, even beneath the exhaustion and travel grime.

"Well, well, little sunstar. Let the games begin."

CHAPTER 5
VALLA

Valla was nodding off over a plate long scraped clean when an older woman approached her. She had a face craggy as a gargoyle's, and her hair was twisted into a vicious bun. Her eyes were steely flints.

"I'm Hearthkeeper Frieda. I understand you're my new charge. Come, southerner. You need to stop drinking and go to bed, or you will regret it on the morrow. My lord's servants rise with the wind."

"But the wind here never sleeps," Valla muttered.

"Exactly."

Valla rose and stretched, waving a sleepy goodbye to Astrid before trailing off after Frieda. The woman was silent as stone and just as resistant to Valla's attempts at small talk.

She followed Frieda through the kitchens to a barracks-style living quarters. Baggy straw mattresses lined cold, lifeless stone walls.

Valla stilled. Apparently her fiancé's idea of hospitality was a chilly, damp hovel beneath the kitchens. A single woodstove burned low on the far end of the room, where the other poor cretins who'd been banished to Frieda's service slept. They clustered as close as they could to the glowing stove, and they all wore more layers than Valla. It was almost enough to make her rethink her ruse.

Frieda pointed her gnarled finger toward an empty mattress. Valla grabbed it by the corner and began dragging it towards the stove. The dragon's milk hadn't done nearly enough to banish the memory of the cold burrowed deep in her bones.

Frieda snatched the back of Valla's shirt.

Valla whirled on the woman. "How dare—"

She broke off. What had she been about to say? How dare she grab her like that? She was no one here—less than no one, given their prejudice against her people.

"What do you think you're doing?" Frieda rasped.

"Sleeping?"

"Those closest to the fire are those who've served my lord the longest. You have not earned your spot. I don't know what that sun brat let you get away with, but that's over while you're my charge."

Valla closed her eyes and counted to ten. She was far too close to snapping and revealing her identity.

She gave Frieda a short nod. "I understand." Humility was proving to be a hard-learnt lesson.

Frieda gripped her chin and sunk her blunt nails into Valla's windchapped skin. "If you understand, say, 'Yes, Hearthkeeper Frieda.'"

Valla fisted her hands and squeezed. "Yes, Hearthkeeper." She tried to tear away, but Frieda's grip tightened, digging into her skin hard enough to bruise.

"Say it properly, girl. You will learn to follow my directions to the letter."

Valla shoved down every self-important bone in her body and spoke through clenched teeth. "Yes, Hearthkeeper Frieda."

Frieda finally relented, tutting and releasing Valla's face. She turned her attentions to two girls curled up by the wall, whispering to one another.

Valla released a shaky breath and massaged her sore jaw. What the fuck had she gotten herself into?

She shook out the lumpy mattress and lay down on it. The straw was fresh, at least, but it was a far cry from the goose-down and silk she was used to. She didn't even have a blanket.

Valla curled around herself and squinched her eyes shut, conjuring to mind sweltering summer nights in the Sun Palace when she'd have sold her soul for a glass of ice water. The sooner she got off this mountain, the better.

VALLA WOKE to muscles on fire. Her back and neck were stiff from the thin mattress and stone floor, and her legs still ached from her trek through the deep snow. She should have asked Rodrick for time to recover, but she'd been too caught up in her lie.

An odd feeling came over her, and she blinked her eyes open. Frieda stood above her mattress, staring down at her like a fierce, beady-eyed bird.

"You may lounge about in the south, but in Frostheim we rise with the sun, as the moon is not so friendly."

Valla stumbled to her feet and rubbed the sleep from her eyes.

Frieda thrust an empty tray into her hands. "Bring the lord his tea. Make sure there's sugar. He takes sugar with it."

Valla trudged up the stone steps to the kitchens and loaded the tray with cup, kettle, and a tiny dish of sugar cubes. If only she had a bit of poison to dissolve in the brew.

"Ought to bring two cups," a kitchen maid brushed by her and murmured.

Valla ignored her and headed for Rodrick's rooms, pointed in the right direction by the guards littered throughout the keep. His bedroom was at the end of a long stone hallway lit with torches. Two guards flanked the double doors. Both held their spears upright, unsheathed and ready to use.

She paused in the hallway and poured the tea. The steam wafting off the hot, fragrant liquid made her long for a sip. She debated adding the sugar, but she'd check with him first to see how many he took. She hated it when the palace servants over-sweetened her coffee.

Valla marched forward and rapped on the door. One of the guards glanced at her and laughed. "I wouldn't be going in there right now, Miss."

"Frieda told me to bring his tea."

The guard shrugged. "Do what ye will. Door's unlocked. He's likely abed still."

Valla pushed the door open and stepped inside. She froze as it thunked shut behind her.

Rodrick and a woman were in a tangle of naked limbs atop a pile of furs. The one fur draped haphazardly over them hid little. Valla's cheeks burned. That might have been her warming his furs, had she told him the truth yesterday. Not that that was what she wanted. *Not at all.*

Valla cleared her throat and moved to stand in front of the giant fire blazing in the hearth, letting it warm her backside. She couldn't suppress the small moan that escaped as the fire's glow warmed her stiff muscles.

Rodrick rolled over, fur sliding dangerously low on his hips. A line of dark golden hair trailed up to his navel. He was chiseled with muscle and covered in various scars. His skin looked flush and warm. Was it even possible to be cold, curled up against that expanse of naked flesh?

The woman in his bed was long and lean and pale, twined around Rodrick's more tan skin. All things Valla wasn't.

She couldn't fault him. She'd taken lovers of her own before leaving for Frostheim, eager for any experience outside marital monogamy with the enemy. But it still burned her pride to see. For all he knew, his intended was freezing to death in the ever-raging blizzard outside his gates or buried lifeless beneath the snow.

Valla shook her head and cleared her throat louder. "My lord."

Rodrick sat up in bed and stretched. The woman murmured in her sleep.

"Valla. What are you doing here?" His voice was deep and sleep-thick, his gaze still unguarded and warm as he woke. Valla was surprised he remembered her name.

"Frieda told me to bring you tea."

"You might have left it outside."

"My apologies."

Rodrick crooked a finger at her, and Valla stepped forward like she'd been pulled on a string. The man was hypnotic. She stopped at the side of the bed, and her new vantage point revealed the heavy shadow between his thighs, just beneath the edge of the fur.

Rodrick caught her looking and smirked. "Would you like to join us? You're looking rather blue."

Valla swallowed her spit. *Yes.* "No!"

Rodrick grabbed the teacup and took a swig before Valla could stop him. He spat it out, spraying her with droplets.

"Sigurd's beard, woman. You call this tea? Did you use *any* sugar?"

Valla wiped a drop of liquid off her forehead and flicked it off her fingers. "I'd *planned* to ask how much sugar you took."

"As much as I bloody can. I don't even like tea, but Frieda insists." Rodrick upended the entire saucer of sugar cubes into his teacup, and it threatened to spill over at the edges. "Bah. It's gone too cold to melt them quickly. You'll do better tomorrow, Valla, or I'll have you assigned to the dog kennels."

Valla grit her teeth. He didn't even like the tea! Why was he riding her about it? And she had no desire to be confronted with his lovers every morning. She pasted on a smile.

"I've a fondness for dogs. I think I'd find them better company." Rodrick's white monstrosity of a pet currently slumbered at the foot of his bed, snoring.

He smiled. "Good. Then we'll get along just fine. Now let me resume my morning as the gods intended." He slid an arm around his bedmate's back, nuzzling against her neck, and Valla fled the room.

She returned to Frieda, who sent her to scrub hearths for the rest of the day with a clump of metal wire that bit into her flesh. It seemed a pointless task, much like making one's bed. Scrub a hearth clean so a new fire could be lit in it immediately, in a place where fires stayed lit all year long. Her fiancé must not want excess soot staining his many white furs. By day's end, Valla's lower back ached from hunching over the hearths, and her fingers were red and raw as a blistering sunburn.

That night, she fell asleep immediately, despite the uncomfortable sleeping conditions. When she woke, the chamber's chill had sunk even deeper into her bones, and it was a struggle to uncurl her fingers. Her hands would look like Frieda's before long.

Her lower back twinged when she rose from the floor and limped to the kitchens. She fetched Rodrick's tea and brought it to his rooms, her eyes still thick with sleep crud. This time when she opened his door, he was the only one beneath his furs. Still nude, though, based on the curve of muscular buttocks lit by the glow of the fire.

He had a massive sleigh-style bed, and the dark wood of

the head and footboard was carved with the scene of a wolf pack in full sprint, chasing down something just out of sight. Yesterday she'd been too distracted by his bedmate to notice it.

Valla cleared her throat, and Rodrick rolled over in bed and stretched his arms out in a yawn before settling them behind his head. The tuft of armpit hair his pose exposed was oddly attractive in a primal, male sort of way. He slid his eyes open and ran that electric gaze over her. It was the pose of a man inviting her into his bed, and she was tempted to say yes, if only to feel how warm it must be beneath his furs, curled up against his naked body. No man should be that rugged and enticing at the same time. It wasn't fair.

"Good morning, Valla." His morning voice was like raspy velvet. It curled around her ears and slid down her throat.

Valla bowed her head. "My lord."

"You may call me Rodrick in private. I don't go for all the pomp of the southerners."

"You sleep deeply, Rodrick."

"Maybe I was just giving you a chance to look your fill."

Valla rolled her eyes toward the ceiling. "You wish."

He chuckled, and his face lit with a grin. "Have you brought me my tea, or just come to warm yourself in front of my fire?"

She shoved the tray toward him. "I already put the sugar in."

Rodrick wrapped his hand around the entire teacup, disregarding the handle altogether, and took a swig. His mouth twisted, face contorting in disgust before he spit it back into the cup. "What in the frozen hells did you do to this tea? It tastes like Sigurd's taint."

Valla frowned, all innocence. "Oh, drat. The salt and sugar were right beside one another. I must have gotten them mixed up."

"Ugh." He fell back onto his pillows. "The tea was bad enough without you conspiring to ruin it."

"Why drink it, then? What would you prefer to have in the mornings?"

"Frieda insists it's good for me, but I've a terrible weakness for coffee after spending time in Isaana. I've a difficult time convincing myself to leave the furs without it."

Valla's eyes widened. Coffee beans were only grown in the south, and it was one of Isaana's most profitable exports. It was one of the things she'd dreaded most about coming here; she'd assumed they wouldn't have any, given the trade disputes.

"You have coffee here?"

"You look as if I've promised you the sun."

She tried to keep the eagerness out of her voice. "I could start preparing that for you instead." The corner of her mouth lifted. "And I won't tell Frieda if you let me have some as well." Anything to warm up the bitter mornings.

Rodrick tsked. "Extorting the Storm King. A fine way to be given icicle duty."

Valla's face fell, and Rodrick sighed. "I'm kidding. I'd love for you to bring me coffee instead of that tepid leaf water. I never quite got the knack for preparing it like they do in the south."

"I—it would help me greatly in my chores, due to its energizing effect."

"You shall have it then."

CHAPTER 6

RODRICK

When Valla arrived in Rodrick's room on her third morning in his home, she brought the delicious scent of coffee with her.

Rodrick had crates of the beans smuggled in before his bride arrived, enough to last all winter. He knew what it was like to be in a strange place without the comforts of home, and he'd hoped to bring her some small semblance of that.

He liked that she entered his rooms without knocking. It showed spirit. She behaved like she already belonged here. It also showed how little she knew of the behavior of servants. Would others grow suspicious of her, or chalk it up to Isaanan oddities?

There were shadows beneath her eyes this morning, and her face was chalky. He'd have to check in with Frieda, make sure she wasn't pushing the girl too hard.

Valla passed him a cup from her tray. He blew on the steaming liquid before taking a sip. It was smooth, sweet, and bold. Perfectly balanced. His eyes fluttered shut. "Ah. Delicious. I could kiss you right now."

Valla blushed and glanced away. She took a sip from her own cup, and the little groan of pleasure she made sent a pulse of heat straight to his cock. He readjusted his furs.

"That would be highly improper," she said, batting her eyes at him over the rim of her mug. "But you don't seem a stranger to impropriety."

Rodrick swallowed. He hadn't meant for her to see him with Svana. He'd expected Frieda to let the girl rest for a day before beginning her work, but he shouldn't have been surprised. Frieda had the mountain's will and a temperament as harsh as its weather.

"How are you finding the north?"

"Cold."

"You will learn to like it."

Valla's lips twisted. "I sincerely doubt that."

He nodded towards the hand she had wrapped around the ceramic mug. Her fingers were red and raw, the beginnings of blisters forming on her knuckles and the pads of her fingers.

"You have the hands of a pleasure maid, not a servant."

Valla blanched. "My...my family recently fell on hard times. I was new to the princess's employ."

"A fledgling maid was assigned to serve the princess?"

Valla's lips tightened. "I was her friend."

"You should know that we've found no sign of her or her guards in the snow. The bodies may not emerge till spring."

Valla cast her eyes at her feet. "I feared that would be the case."

Rodrick stifled his frown. Either she was talented at deception, or she genuinely felt bad about their fates. Just how talented a liar was the little sunstar?

"Your princess. What was she like?"

Valla glanced toward the fire. "She was never given the freedom to truly know herself. I pitied her."

"A commonality amongst royalty, I fear."

She gazed up into his eyes. "And you? Did you want to marry her?"

Rodrick shrugged. "I didn't know her. I agreed on behalf of my people."

"But why? You were winning the war."

"We would have won, eventually. But the longer we warred, the more innocents on both sides of the conflict suffered. I have no desire to conquer the south, but I won't let my people starve. We lose more of our farmable land to early winter every year. I only want a piece to cultivate, or an agreement to trade crops."

Valla looked down at her hands and twisted them together. "And now that the princess is gone? Have you written to the king to tell him?"

"Soon. Tell me, Valla, which of the remaining sisters would make a better wife?" He was goading her on purpose. Poking at the edges of her resolve.

"You really intend to—"

"Those were the terms of the alliance."

Valla scoffed. "Perhaps her fate was not so ill-favored."

Rodrick rose an eyebrow. "You think her better off dead?"

"What sort of life is one without choice?"

He raised his coffee mug to her in a toast. "Touché."

"Would you really embark on another engagement so soon? With Seraphina's whereabouts still unknown?"

"If she's not here, she's dead. My people found no trace of her or the guardsmen. Few could Jotunfjall in winter this long without supplies, especially a spoiled Sunstar. You were lucky to make it here without losing any fingers or toes to Sigurd's bite.

"Forgive my impertinence—"

Not likely.

"—but I do not think either of her sisters would suit you, my lord. You seem like a good king. But I'm not so sure you are a good man."

Rodrick's lips curled. "You're right. I'm not. And you'd do well to remember that."

CHAPTER 7

VALLA

Valla hated the cold. It was unshakable. The air was dry as bone, and working for Frieda was enough to make Valla wish she'd died in the avalanche. The idea of going to Rodrick and confessing crossed her mind a few hundred times a day. He already suspected something was amiss. She was no great actress, and her body told its own truths.

Would he believe her? She'd abandoned anything that might identify her in the snow, barring the brand on her hip. And she'd come so far already. She just had to focus, persevere—how much longer could winter last, really?

Recovering enough to descend the mountain while in Frieda's care would be nigh impossible. The woman was relentless. Valla worked from sunup till sundown, day-in and day-out, with no breaks. Her only sustenance was tasteless porridge with a few meager chunks of meat. The reality of her new existence was sobering. She hadn't worked this hard a day in her life, even the summer she spent obsessed with horses and lived at the palace stables.

She served a stint in the kitchens, where she kneaded

dough and churned butter until her arms were limp as noodles and her fingers locked up. Her wrists throbbed. Her back ached from stooping to scrub floors and hearths and dust beneath beds.

Rodrick's hound often found Valla during her chores, getting underfoot and making a mess, including one notable instance where the animal's thrashing tail upended a bucket of dirty water onto a thick rug. The furry monster had proceeded to track muddy pawprints across the flagstone Valla had just scrubbed clean. At least she'd been spared the task of cleaning up the beast's endless shedding. It'd be like trying to bottle snowflakes in a blizzard.

Valla's hands swelled into a mass of fluid-filled blisters, and she had to rip off scraps of fabric from her ragged, filthy travel dress and wrap her hands in them to keep going. Still, the slightest pressure against the blisters stung, and more than a few burst from pressure, fluid leaking into the fabric and crusting together. Her hands hurt enough to distract her from the cold. At least until she lay in bed at night, wrapped up tight in the thin blanket she'd nicked from a room she'd cleaned.

Her dreams were feverish. She developed a rattling cough in her chest, and she shivered herself to sleep every night, glaring at the woodstove whose warmth barely reached her. She didn't ask Frieda for a reprieve. It was clear to her what the head hearthkeeper's answer would be, and Valla refused to give her the pleasure of seeing her beg.

Valla's list of duties this morning included scrubbing cauldrons large enough to cook a toddler in, feeding chickens that pecked at her ankles and hands mercilessly, and mucking out stalls with the stablehands. She suffered no delusions that she was being treated fairly. The other girls worked the kitchens or cleaned the keep, which was hard work, but they were regu-

larly done long before her, and there was always companionship and a warm fire to be had.

Her morning coffee visits with Rodrick were the single
bright spot in her day. She enjoyed them more than she cared
to admit. She didn't find any more women in his bed, and
their manner with each other grew easier by the day.

Valla swayed on her feet as she climbed the stairs to
Rodrick's room for her morning visit. She had to pause more
than once to lean against the handrail and wait for her vision
to stop wavering and leaking black at the edges.

He wasn't in his room when she arrived. She set the coffee
down and eyed the bed piled high with furs with envy, half-
tempted to lie down and take a nap. Even just sitting propped
up against the headboard to rest her weary, aching feet was
tempting, but it'd be far too easy to fall asleep. There was an
armchair in front of his fire draped in furs, as everything
belonging to him was. His stamp of ownership. *Rodrick,
Rodrick, Rodrick.* Slayer and skinner of white-furred things.

Valla scooted the armchair closer to the fire and sat down in
it, curling her legs up beneath her. She wasn't allowed this close
to a fire's warmth unless she was visiting Rodrick in the mornings or stealing a moment while stoking a hearth. The chair was
soft and warm and drenched in his scent. The flames danced back
and forth, swaying hypnotically, and Valla fought to stay awake.

Rodrick

RODRICK RETURNED to his rooms to change after his early
morning ice bath. He paused when he saw the dark cloud of
hair cresting the top of his chair. She was nestled so deep in his
furs that her face was barely visible, wrapped up like a cocoon.

Her skin was wan beneath the dusky eyelashes sweeping the tops of her cheeks.

Their coffee sat beside her, long gone cold. "Valla," he whispered.

She didn't respond.

He brushed a finger across her cheek. "Valla."

Her face crinkled in upset, and she wormed her way deeper into the furs.

He couldn't help but smile. His treacherous, treacherous smile. He liked returning to his rooms and finding her occupying his space, like she was relaxed and at home.

He'd kept a close eye on her as she toiled around the keep. Frieda was working her at a grueling pace. If it continued, she'd find her way into an early grave. Surely she would break and tell him the truth soon. He'd noticed the raw redness around her fingers, the hesitancy in her body when she bent over. The sharp intake of breath when she stretched for something just out of her reach. The girl was spent. Not that his hearthkeeper would care. She used and abused the servants, molding them into tough little things hewn from rock.

Rodrick frowned when he noticed the mottling of a dark bruise at Valla's hairline. From the avalanche, judging by the aged coloring.

He scooped her up in his arms, bundle of furs and all, and carried her to his bed. He expected her to stir and protest, but she curled into his pillow with a sleepy murmur and began to breathe deep once more. He could get used to seeing her in his bed.

He smoothed a hand over the small of Valla's back, letting a faint trickle of his magic flow into her. The cold would soothe some of the inflammation in her muscles.

Nanook hopped onto the bed and curled up at the girl's feet, shooting a disapproving look at Rodrick.

He arched an eyebrow at the hound. "You don't usually

take to strangers." Valla likely smelled like him from her time in his furs. Odd, how much the idea pleased him.

Nanook rested her head on her paws and thumped her tail against the bed.

Rodrick shook his head and left her to her sleep.

CHAPTER 8
VALLA

Valla dreamed for the first time since she'd left the south. Flashes of fire and snow and devilish scars over crinkled grins and his *scent*. His scent crawled up her nose and down her throat and settled in her belly. Warm and basking and so, so comfortable. She stretched and blinked her eyes open, mildly disoriented when she didn't see the painted ceiling of her bedroom in the Sun Palace overhead. Instead there were timber beams and stone and white fur tickling her nose—and that accursed scent.

Valla sat up with a jerk, her heart pounding. She'd fallen asleep. How long had it been? Far too long, judging by the dream and how rested she felt and the fire banked low in the hearth.

Too long by half, when Rodrick asked, "Sleep well, dear?" from his position in the chair by the hearth.

She glanced down. *She was in his bed?* Had she moved there on her own?

"I, I—"

"Relax. I moved you to the bed. You looked like you could use the rest."

"Oh sunmother. Frieda's going to kill me. I'm so sorry, my lord."

"It's alright, Valla. Though I'm glad you woke. I was beginning to wonder if I'd have to sleep in my chair."

She jerked her eyes up to him. "What time is it?"

"Evening meal was two hours ago."

"Fuck!" Valla scrambled from the bed. But her feet were still tangled in the furs, and she careened face-first toward the floor.

Rodrick snapped his arm out toward her, and a blue beam of frost shot into her chest.

Her descent abruptly stopped as cold flooded her body, ice rushing into her lungs. She tried to blink and couldn't. Even her eyelids were frozen.

She teetered forward, the icy roots she'd grown beginning to crack under her weight. Rodrick strode forward and righted her. With a sweep of his hand across her frozen cheek, he recalled his magic, the sparking blue frost flowing back into his fingertips.

She clenched the front of his shirt and took a halting breath, the air in her lungs a ball of piercing fire.

"You—" she gasped. "Don't ever do that to me again! I'd rather fall on my face." How many of her countrymen had he frozen into a similar state, stuck staring, ice-eyed, as the lord of winter approached to deliver their deaths.

"And I would rather you did not."

Rodrick was gripping her waist, keeping her steady. He looked down at her hands still fisted in his shirt and frowned.

"Your hands." He circled her wrists and lowered her back to the bed. He began unraveling the dirty wraps, and Valla swatted him away.

"*Stop.* I don't need your help."

He caught her arms in his iron grip and raised a stern

eyebrow. "You obviously do, since you refuse to ask for it yourself. Have you shown Frieda?"

Valla scoffed. "She's well aware, I'm sure."

He resumed unwrapping the makeshift bandages, and Valla winced as the fabric crusted to her raw skin pulled away.

Rodrick sucked in a breath. "Fuck, Valla. Have you been working like this?"

"It's fine. And I've hardly a choice in the matter, have I?"

His frown tightened. "It's not *fine*." He turned her hands over, inspecting them with light touches. "Let me help you."

"And how do you propose to do that?"

"My magic. I can't heal them, but the cold will help the swelling."

Valla shook her head vehemently. "I've had enough of your ice inside me for a lifetime."

"I can make it gentle. It was harsh before because I was reacting on reflex. I didn't temper it."

All she knew of Rodrick's magic were the tales soldiers brought back from the battlefield. That he froze impassable rivers and shattered metal swords—how he hardened men's flesh to ice before he ran them through. Did he make it quick, at least? Or let them linger? She shut down her spiraling train of thought. He wasn't going to hurt her—probably.

He gripped her chin with gentle fingers and lifted her eyes to his. "Trust me."

Valla sighed. Her hands hurt enough at this point to try almost anything. "Okay."

Rodrick's silver eyes glowed, his hands against her skin growing colder. Before, his magic had been a swift plunge into icy water. Now it was the caress of first frost, a flurry of snowflakes on eyelashes before the blizzard began in earnest.

It was concentrated in her hands at first, then eddies of power began snaking through her body, seeking out all the aching parts of her. The hair on her arms rose as his magic skated down her spine to her lower back, then trailed down to the taut arches of her feet. Her curls floated at the edge of her vision, eddies of air lifting them off her shoulders.

A vein pulsed in Rodrick's forehead. Using his magic like this must require a great degree of control. Lightning danced in his eyes as he scoured her face for a reaction.

Valla stared past him at a spot on the wall. She didn't like that he held the key to easing her suffering when he'd been the cause of it to begin with.

"Well? How do you feel?"

"It would seem the cold isn't all bad," she begrudgingly admitted. "But perhaps if your servants weren't treated so abominably to begin with, this wouldn't be necessary."

"You're right."

She looked back at him. "What?"

"I said you're right. This is my responsibility. I'll talk to her."

Valla bit the inside of her cheek. He wasn't supposed to be *nice* when she lashed out. Wasn't supposed to keep defying her expectations. Much more, and she'd have to begin reforming her entire idea of him.

"Thank you."

He graced her with a small smile and recalled his magic. This time, its absence left her feeling bereft. Like she'd lost a little piece of him.

"Any time you want me, you need but only ask."

CHAPTER 9
VALLA

Frieda wasn't around when Valla returned to the hovel beneath the kitchens, all her chores incomplete. It was a brief mercy, and she tossed all night, anxiety roiling in her belly at the prospect of facing the hearthkeeper come morning.

She rose early and hurried to the kitchens. Frieda was barking orders at the cooks, but her eagle eyes zeroed in on Valla as soon as she entered the room.

Bile rose in Valla's throat.

She prepared the coffee in record time, keeping her eye's down lest she meet Frieda's gaze. She set the tray and scuttled for the exit.

"Where do you think you're going, Valla?" Frieda's tone was acerbic.

Valla gulped. "To take the king his tea."

Frieda swept across the kitchen. Her black skirt was perfectly tailored to cover her feet without brushing the ground when she walked. It made her look like a floating matron of doom.

"Where were you all day yesterday?"

"In and out of the privy. All the porridge disagrees with me."

"One of the maids told me she saw you leaving my lord's quarters in the evening."

"I left my tray there and went to fetch it."

Frieda's gaze swiveled to the tray Valla was carrying.

"And *why* do you have two cups?"

Valla flashed her a saccharin smile. "I've been bringing him twice the tea. He's grown fond of it lately."

The corner of Frieda's lip lifted, exposing a long canine yellow with age.

"That's twice you've lied to me this morning, girl. There won't be a third." Frieda lifted the lid of the teapot. Valla's fingers tightened around the tray.

"This isn't my tea blend."

"No, it isn't."

Frieda made a loud whistling sound between her teeth. "And who told you to serve the king coffee instead of my tea? Serving yourself as well, by the looks of it."

Valla stared at her feet and bit her cheek, resisting the urge to slam the silver tray into Frieda's face. The hearthkeeper had a special talent for testing her resolve.

"Rodrick did, ma'am."

She didn't see the slap coming.

Her head snapped to the side, the flare of pain delayed. The tray fell, ceramic shattering and hot coffee splashing everywhere.

"You dare use the Storm King's given name? Insolent whelp."

Valla wasn't usually one to cry, but the last two weeks had been *a lot*. Moisture welled in her eyes, and she clenched her blistered hands into fists to keep the tears from falling. Her cheek was still hot with the slap.

"Clean this up. You will no longer serve the king in the

mornings. You've been far too pleased with yourself lately, and I didn't have you serve him so you could dally the day away drinking that bitter bean juice and ogling him. He'd never take the likes of you to bed, if that's what you've in mind. It's a blessing from Sigurd that that southern brat was buried in the snows, and I'll be even happier when the thaw comes and you can return from whence you came."

Valla's tears escaped as she knelt and began scraping the ceramic shards into a pile. They ran down her face in dirty streaks. "What would you have me do instead, Hearthkeeper?"

"You will go with Herja and Rani to scrape icicles before the blizzard hits."

THE WIND WAS fiercer today than it'd been on the day of the avalanche. Valla could feel the oncoming storm in the weight of the air. She frowned up at the snow-capped peak stretching beyond the keep's walls.

Valla thought icicle duty was a cautionary tale. The task they threatened servants with to get them to behave. How wrong she was.

"Rodrick must be on one," Rani said. She was a thin girl with dishwater blonde hair that assisted the cooks.

"Why do you say that?" Valla asked.

"He bears the frost heart. People say his emotion affects the weather."

"Goddess help us all if that's true," Valla muttered.

"And here I thought he'd be elated that bitch died in the snows. Svana was certainly pleased," Herja said.

Valla's lips twisted. Svana, she'd learned, had been the woman beneath Rodrick's furs the first morning she'd attended him.

"You." Herja addressed Valla with a lift of her chin. "You were in her employ. Was she a right cunt?"

"She was a royal. What do you think?"

One thing had become abundantly clear during her stay. Had Valla gone through with the marriage, she would've been queen to people who thought more of the icebear dung caking their snowshoes than her.

"I can't believe Frieda is making us do this," Rani said in a nasal whine.

"What harm are the icicles? Or is Frieda just being sadistic?" Valla asked.

Rani laughed, and Herja shot her a look.

"Those things fall with a sharp point, they can poke a man through the eye. And there's guards stationed near here," Herja said.

"I'd hope the guards know better than to stand beneath icicles during a storm. Or even be *out* during the storm, unlike us," Rani said.

Valla followed the girls to a tall archway studded with long spikes of ice. The ice here had a mind of its own. It was malevolent, freezing into razor sharp shards that drew blood with a prick.

A rickety wooden ladder rested against the fortress wall. Valla rubbed her hands together and shuffled in place, trying to keep her body warm. "What'd you two do to get sent here?"

Herja sneered and passed her the long metal scythe she'd brought. "Someone's got to hold your ladder. Hurry up. I don't want to be out here when the storm hits."

Valla glanced at the sky. Dark clouds boiled around the mountain, and a persistent stream of flurries filled her vision. They needed to get this over with quickly, then she'd find some empty, dusty room to light a fire in and warm her bones.

"Alright," Valla said, eyeing the ladder. "Hold me steady."

The girls took up positions on either side of the ladder. Valla stepped onto the first rung and cursed. The wood was slick with ice. She climbed one-handed, her other hand gripping the long, unwieldy scythe. Her blistered fingertips stuck to the ice, and it burned each time she had to tug them away.

Valla's life flashed before her eyes each time her smooth-soled shoes lost traction. She needed a pair of spiked boots like the guards wore, but Frieda hadn't exactly been forthcoming with new wardrobe pieces. It'd been all she could do to convince the laundresses to wash her travel clothes.

Herja and Rani snickered each time Valla nearly slipped. She paused and took a deep breath, trying to banish her fear. Her left hand ached from her death-grip on the ladder.

Valla grit her teeth and stepped up to the final rung. She leaned out with the scythe to swipe at the icicles, clinging to the ladder with her other arm. Several broke free with a crack.

Another swipe, and the ladder danced with her movements. The girls had gone quiet. Valla glanced down.

Gone. They were *gone*. Fuck. She needed to make this quick.

The wind picked up speed as the storm neared, shaking the rickety ladder with each blast. Valla struck at the icicles and tried not to look down. She cleared them all, except for one small cluster at the edge of her reach. If she didn't get it, Frieda was liable to find out and give her some other abominable task as punishment. Valla slid over, keeping one foot on the ladder. She gripped the lip of the roof and stretched out her scythe arm. Then another gust came.

The ladder trembled and twisted—and then it was falling out from under her.

Valla screamed and dropped the scythe. She snatched at the roof with her right hand, curling her fingers around the icy buildup. Her arms strained with the struggle of supporting her weight.

"Help!" she screamed, hoping someone could hear. The courtyard was empty, everyone inside due to the approaching storm. There was only the hard ground beneath her and her aching arms. Valla tried to pull herself up onto the roof, but her grip was too slick.

Would the snow cushion her fall? How thick was it? The scythe and icicles were down there somewhere, waiting to slice into her if she fell at the wrong angle.

The cold bit into her bare fingers, and her arms shuddered. Her nails splintered where they dug into the stone.

"Is anyone there? Herja, Rani? Please come back. It's funny, you've had your laugh."

Valla's arms trembled. Her abused fingers were numb against the ice. Her biceps burned.

The wind battered at her. The numbness was spreading down her wrists. Her shoulders stretched white-hot.

Then her arms gave out, and she was falling. Valla clenched her eyes shut and contemplated her life choices.

Glass shattered below her.

Her descent jerked to a stop, her lungs choking on ice. Cold air compressed her, pushing in at the edges. She tried to open her eyes and discovered they were frozen shut.

Is this what death felt like in the north? Her body moved, tugged through the air like she was attached to a rope. Was she ...*floating*?

Definitely dead, then. Likely her soul being yanked toward some hellish afterlife where Frieda reigned.

Warmth wrapped around her. At least it was hot in hell.

"It's okay. I've got you. I have you. You're safe."

The voice was familiar. Valla tried to open her eyes again, and they peeled open, lashes pulling free where they were stuck to her skin.

Rodrick. He held her in his arms, her face cradled to his neck.

Valla's body began to wake back up. Cold wracked her, and she shivered uncontrollably, chattering against his ear. Her clothes were soaked through, like she'd just taken a dip in a lake. A layer of melting ice coated her skin.

Her heartbeat was far slower than it ought to be, and she struggled with her next breath. Like the air was too thick to take in.

Valla pulled back and looked into her savior's eyes. Lightning danced in Rodrick's irises, and he wore a furious expression on his face.

She glanced around. They were in an office, the walls behind a mammoth desk lined with books. Storm winds rushed in from a blown-out window with glass still clinging to the edges of the frame.

Valla buried her face in his neck again, too shaken to worry about appearances. Of course it was he who saved her. That minty pine he exuded flowed off of him and muddled her senses. "Thank you. Thank you."

Rodrick clutched the back of her skull and pulled her tighter against him. "I used my magic—it wasn't gentle. Fuck, we have to warm you up."

Valla clung to him as he carried her out of the office with sure strides. Then they were in an antechamber off of his hall, and he was barking orders at a heavily pregnant woman. "Thyri. Gather help and draw a hot bath in the guest room, as quickly as you can."

CHAPTER 10

RODRICK

Rodrick carried Valla into his rooms and set her on the edge of his bed.

"Your lips are turning blue. I need to get you out of these wet clothes."

"This is h-h-ardly the time for seduction," Valla chattered.

"We need to get you warm before hypothermia sets in. You're shaking like a nude tree. I'm going to disrobe you."

Valla gave a shaky nod.

He was lucky the shock of his magic hadn't killed her outright. He'd been going over appeals at his desk when icicles began raining outside his window. The reality was so absurd, it'd taken him precious moments to realize what was going on. And then her scream, and panic tightening his throat before he shot a blast of frost through the glass that froze her midair. A pillar of ice now extended from his office window to the ground far below.

Rodrick untied Valla's ratty cloak and peeled her sodden shirt up from her waist. She stuck her arms up as he pulled it overhead.

Her dusky rose nipples were hard pebbles, and goosebumps prickled her breasts and abdomen. Her collarbones stuck out sharply. She wasn't eating enough; he'd have to tell the cook to make some southern fare for her.

She folded her arms around her abdomen and shook.

"You aren't wearing nearly enough layers. Where's your coat?"

"These are the only clothes I have."

Rodrick stilled. He knew Frieda had grown willful during his southern campaigns, when she was left to run the keep without him, but this was madness.

Rodrick unlaced Valla's pants and peeled them down her hips, underwear and all. The tuft of dark hair between her legs captured his attention. Her naked, tan flesh swaddled against the pure white of his furs heated his blood.

"You've got me naked. Now what?"

He looked her in the eye. "You might not like it, but the fastest way to thaw you out is skin-to-skin contact with a warm body. You'll absorb my body heat. Are you comfortable with that?"

Valla cast her eyes down his body in a slow perusal. "What makes you think I wouldn't like it?"

He ignored the pulse of heat that shot straight to his cock. She was beautiful, temptation made flesh, but this was about saving her life. She was likely still in shock from the fall.

She stared boldly as he stripped out of his clothes and boots, his cock stiffening every second her gaze lingered on him.

Frostmother have mercy.

The act of sliding beneath his furs with her *right there*, naked and in need of his warmth, nearly undid him. He liked the sight of her curled up in his bed far too much. He had to keep reminding himself that she didn't want to be here, didn't want to marry him. Would leave as soon as spring came. He couldn't keep her.

"I—apologize for my body's reaction. You're a beautiful woman."

Valla crawled up the bed and tucked herself beneath his furs with a smile on her face.

Rodrick stared at his ceiling beams and counted to ten, willing himself to calm. He was behaving like a boy before his first tupping.

He didn't move to touch her at first, but then she coughed, and it was rattling and wet. He slid his arm around her waist and pulled her against him. His large body dwarfed hers. Her shoulder blades pressed into his chest, her icy feet tangling with his calves until they were flush against his skin. He loved the feeling of her smaller form encompassed by his. Protected. Safe. Warm. *His*.

Her plump ass wriggled against him as she situated herself, and his cock went hard as a pike, prodding the cleft of her ass cheeks.

He gripped her hip to still her. "Valla. Please don't fucking do that."

Why the fuck had he done this to himself? This was torture. He was never going to be able to get her out of his head now.

"It's fine, Rodrick. Not the first hard cock I've felt."

Jealousy surged through him. His wife had lain with another? He had no right to expect her innocence—his own was long gone—but it still burned. He was a possessive man.

Valla's dark curls tickled his nose. She smelled like his magic—crisp winter and morning ice. He slid his hands up and down her arms, willing his warmth into her.

"What were you doing out there?"

Valla bristled. "Perhaps you should ask your hearthkeeper."

Rodrick cursed. "She sent you out there in this weather? To cut bloody icicles? And you listened?"

The icicles were cleared regularly, but usually by nimble

chimney sweeps used to the heights and the ice. And always with several people to look out and help. Was Frieda treating Valla this way because she was Isaanan, or did she suspect something more?

Valla stiffened against him. "Did I have any other choice? If I don't contribute or do as she says, you're liable to turn me out in the cold."

His arms tightened around her. "You really think I would do that? What tales they must tell of me in the south. Do I also boil the bones of children and offer them to the storm gods?"

"They tell of a harsh leader who expects much and forgives little."

Rodrick shook his head. "You could have been seriously hurt. Was there no one else with you?"

"There was. They left once I was up the ladder."

"Who?" he growled.

"It doesn't matter. You cannot punish your entire court."

"Watch me."

He would get names out of her sooner or later. He hadn't totally given up on the idea of Valla as his bride, but he was appalled by the behavior of some of his subjects. He needed Valla warm and willing, not counting the days until spring. Had she not been outside his window, she could've fallen and broken her neck or been seriously injured.

He pictured her slowly freezing to death as the blizzard raged outside, the wind muting her cries for help. He'd find her the next day, dark curls peeking out from the snow, her face frozen in an eternal scream. Blue as his mother had been when they'd returned her body—

His magic leaked out of his fingertips, and Valla shivered.

Rodrick's lip curled, and his rubbing grew more vigorous.

"Since Frieda can't be bothered to take care of you, I will. You can serve me instead of her."

Testing his deceitful bride had been a game to him at first, but things had gone too far. At this rate she wouldn't make it to spring. And the more time he spent with her, the more he wanted to get to know her. It was refreshing to interact without the burden of a marriage contract—or a marriage, for that matter—between them.

"Let me guess. I'm to be your personal mop, sponging up all the melted ice your magic leaves about the keep."

Rodrick snorted. "My personal attendant, Thyri, grows heavy with child. She's due to take rest leave any day now, and she won't be returning until the babe is weaned. You could take her place."

"What would attending you entail?"

Stubborn witch.

"It doesn't bloody matter what it entails. If you continue like this, you're going to die on this mountain."

Teeth chattering, she muttered, "I suppose you're right."

"Don't argue with me. Servants aren't supposed to argue with kings."

"Would I still be your personal coffee fetcher?"

"Always. I'll ensure Frieda doesn't bother you while you're in the kitchens. Other tasks would include bringing meals to my quarters, helping with my wardrobe, carrying conveyance and messages and the like. You'd help with Nanook when I'm busy and accompany me on outings. And tend to my furs, of course."

"Is that a euphemism?"

His cock twitched against her ass. "You've a dirty mind. How do you think my furs stay so pristine?"

Valla shrugged. "I assumed you went and hunted some poor new animal every time one got dirty. There are quite a lot of them, after all."

Rodrick rolled his eyes. "You would, wouldn't you?"

She rolled over in his arms, pressing her face into his chest and lining up all the parts of her body that were still cold against him.

The heat of her core and the brush of his cock against the curls of her mons nearly undid him.

"Tell me then."

He blinked down at her, still stunned by the casual intimacy. "What?"

"Tell me about the furs. You can't just roll your eyes and scoff at my lack of knowledge if you're not willing to educate me."

His lips lifted in a smile, and he rested his chin on the top of her head, breathing in her scent.

"It's true that some of the furs come from animals we hunted for food, or predators that strayed from their pack and threatened humans. But most are from treasured pets or livestock. When an animal that's spent its life in our service passes, we don't let its body go to waste. Its meat, its skin, all are given purpose. Its body serves us even in death.

"The lame snow fox my father kept as a pet did not survive him, but one day its fur will swaddle my children as it swaddled me. The winter elk I rode as a toddler will not survive me, but my child will costume themselves with its antlers." He hesitated, sliding a hand down the furs wrapped around them. "The icebear that pulls the warsleds will warm the bed of me and my wife."

Valla was silent for several long seconds.

"That's beautiful."

Her reaction surprised him. He'd expected her to call it morbid, to react with disgust. Southerners often had little appreciation for northern ways. His appreciation for her grew.

"You don't have any children, then? Do you want them?"

"No, I don't have any. Though fatherhood is an expectation that I have ... grown accustomed to."

"So it isn't your babe rounding Thyri's belly?"

Rodrick went cold. The flash of lightning in his eyes splintered the shadows on her skin, and he fought the urge to pull away from her. She was still fighting off the chill of his magic.

"You think so little of me still."

"It wouldn't be uncommon in the Sun Palace ... "

"Perhaps you should leave your southern suppositions where they belong—at the base of my mountain."

She was silent for a few seconds. "You're right. I'm sorry."

Rodrick brows raised. The sunstar, apologizing for her misconceptions? Perhaps they were making progress after all.

"The babe is not mine. Thyri has a lovely husband. The frost heart is not a burden so lightly given."

"That's what they call your magic, right? The one passed down the family line."

"And how would you know that?"

Valla stiffened in his arms, her heartbeat speeding up. "The servants speak of it, and the princess mentioned it to me on our journey here. It seems a useful tool. You've saved me with it twice now."

"Useful, yes, but not without its costs. I cannot spend too long away from Frostheim."

"Why not? What will happen?"

He debated telling her. It was sensitive information to give the daughter of his enemy, especially when she was not yet his wife.

"The legend of the frost heart hails from a time when dragons still roamed the skies. It speaks of my ancestor slaying a dragon and eating her heart to inherit her icy breath. Ice dragons, as you might imagine, did not fare well far from their natural habitat. If I'm away from the north for too long, I will weaken and eventually die. It's what killed my mother."

"But your campaigns in the Isaana—"

"Were effective but short-lived, and close to the border. I

left my generals in charge if I needed to return to the mountain for a time."

"I had no idea."

"It's not common knowledge, for obvious reasons."

"The other servants say your emotions affect the weather. Was the lack of coffee this morning so bad? Or do I have stress over your impending nuptials to blame for that avalanche?"

Rodrick laughed. "When I was younger and had less control, sometimes they would. People dreaded my tantrums. But this is just Frostheim in winter."

Valla's upper body was warm, so he moved lower, stroking her hip. His fingers ran across a large, raised scar, and Valla went stock-still.

"Does it still pain you?" The wound must have been significant to scar so badly, though it was in an odd place. Perhaps a fall?

"Not physically."

Rodrick didn't inquire further. He was patient, and she was already opening to him like a hothouse flower. She would tell him when she was ready. He moved his hand lower, stroking her outer thigh. His touch was less about warmth now and more about sensation.

"So which brilliant man came up with this method for getting a woman naked?"

He snorted. "The first thing a Frostheim warrior learns is how to survive in the cold. And the shared heat of two bodies is one of the quickest ways to get warm. You've nothing to be ashamed of. I've been in many a pile of naked soldiers, all shivering against one another. The north laughs at modesty. When there's ice in your beard and your eyes begin to crunch if you go too long without blinking, you'll have no patience for propriety."

"That sounds miserable."

"Aye. Though I still prefer it to your land. The first time I journeyed south, I thought less clothes was the answer. I woke the next day with skin stinging and pink as sugar apples. Some of my soldiers had blisters atop their shoulders so swollen it hurt them to wear clothes. And the *bugs. That* was misery."

Rodrick's door swung open, and they both froze. Thyri's eyes went wide before she averted her gaze to the corner of the room. "The bath is ready, my lord."

"Thank you, Thyri. You can go now."

Valla tugged the furs over her head and groaned. "News of this will be all over the keep now."

"Thyri's a good lass."

"That doesn't mean she doesn't like to gossip."

Rodrick swung out of the bed and quickly dressed. Then he picked her up, bundle of furs and all.

"I can walk."

"Your clothes are soaking wet, and the bath is right down the hall. So unless you'd prefer to go in my clothes—"

"Fine," Valla grumbled, tucking herself so deep inside the blankets that only the top of her head was exposed.

CHAPTER II

VALLA

Rodrick carried Valla to a room just one door down from his. A large copper tub steamed in the corner. The room was richly decorated but free of personal effects. One of Rodrick's signature white furs was draped across the foot of the bed, and he set her down on the edge of it.

"Whose rooms are these?"

"No one's."

"They're quite finely decorated for not belonging to anyone. And I know that's not the northern way."

Rodrick sighed, a small smile creeping onto his face. "You're learning. These rooms were meant for Princess Seraphina. You can stay in them while you're attending me."

Valla's eyes snapped open. Giving his betrothed's rooms to a maid? Did he suspect her? Had he recognized the shape of the brand on her hip?

Surely he would have said something.

"I can't stay here."

"Why not?"

"I'm a servant. What would people think?"

"Allowances can be made. While I do expect you to earn your keep, you're still a guest in my court. And you've been treated poorly. Worse than poorly. My carelessness nearly got you killed."

"Won't people talk?"

Rodrick shrugged. "Do you care? You don't plan on staying, after all."

Valla chewed her lip. She was surprised to realize she did care about the opinions of the Frostheimers, but returning to her sad mattress on the edge of the Frieda's warren, when he was offering her this... She couldn't do it. She was only capable of being so magnanimous.

"I'll need you close by if you're going to be attending me," Rodrick added.

"Right. Okay."

He smiled. "Get in the bath while it's hot. You still look like you've been touched by the Frostmother. I'll be back."

He left, and Valla shrugged off the furs and scurried for the tub. The fire in the room had been lit recently, and the stone floors were still chilly. She dipped a toe into the water to test the temperature, then climbed in and sunk down until water covered her shoulders.

Her fiancé was nothing like she'd expected. She was warming to him, much to her chagrin. Agreeing to be his personal attendant was beyond reckless. She should be distancing herself, not living and working right under his nose. Her disguise was precarious enough as it was. The brand had been a close call—too close.

If Rodrick discovered her ruse before spring, how would he react? Would he still insist on marrying her? The Storm King was growing on her, but Frostheim decidedly wasn't. If anything, living here had confirmed her fears that she'd never truly be accepted by the northerners.

There was a soft knock on the door, and Rodrick entered carrying a tray with two cups of coffee on it.

Valla groaned. "You magnificent bastard."

"I'm quite legitimate, thank you." Rodrick set the tray down and passed her a cup. "I don't make it as well as you, but I did my best."

She took a sip and sighed as the heat curled into her belly. "It's good."

"I missed you this morning. You didn't bring our coffee."

Our coffee, not *his* coffee.

Valla gulped as tears rose in her throat. Which was ridiculous. She did *not* cry—especially not twice in one day. Her father had trained her out of it early. And there was no bloody reason to be crying right now, but the stress that'd been knotting up in her body for weeks was all coming loose beneath the hot water. And Rodrick was being so fucking nice, and all she'd done was lie to him.

Were their situations reversed, her father would have killed a wayward northern servant. Or tortured them for information on their master.

Concern passed over his face, and he knelt beside the tub. "What? What is it? Are you hurt?"

She shook her head and wiped away the snot leaking from her nose. "Just overwhelmed. I'm sorry. I don't know why I'm crying."

Rodrick took her mug from her. He circled the tub, pulled up a stool behind her, and sat. "You're in shock still. Your body has been through a lot. Here, lean back."

She sunk back against the rim of the tub.

Rodrick drew her head into his hands and began massaging her temples. Valla was half-convinced she'd hit her head, and this was all a wild fever dream. His body was temptation, but his hands—his hands were sinful.

"Relax your jaw."

She hadn't been aware it was tense, but when she consciously let go, her breaths came easier.

His hands sunk into her hair, strong fingers digging and pulling at her scalp. He massaged the knots in her shoulders and the cords of her neck until her head lolled in his hands. Valla closed her eyes and breathed deep. She could live in this moment.

Rodrick carefully untangled his fingers from her hair without pulling any of the knots her curls were prone to.

"Better?"

Valla gave a sleepy nod. "Frieda forbade me from bringing you the coffee. She's quite set on that tea—are you sure she isn't poisoning you?"

He gave a light snort.

"You are not what she—the princess—expected."

Rodrick's hands stilled on her shoulders. "How's that?"

Valla was treading on dangerous ground. "You're...caring. I don't think she had many caring people in her life.".

He grunted. "I'll leave you to it so you can bathe. The room is yours. I'll have Thyri bring you dry clothes."

"What will my duties tomorrow be?"

Rodrick frowned. "You've got a bad cough and had quite the shock. Take a few days; let me know when you're feeling better."

CHAPTER 12
VALLA

The clothes Rodrick had delivered were not the clothes of a servant. They weren't as sumptuous as what Valla would wear in Isaana—or what she imagined Frostheim's queen would dress in—but they were certainly better quality than she'd seen the other servants wearing.

There were thick, dyed wool dresses and fur-lined cloaks. Sets of undergarments meant to layer beneath her clothes to better insulate from the cold. An assortment of gloves, from soft leather to knit mittens lined with fur on the inside. Boots, snowshoes, and even cozy slippers for walking around the bedroom. The most stunning piece was a heavy crimson cloak trimmed with white fur around the collar.

"These clothes are too fine for a servant," she told Rodrick when he checked in on her later that day.

He shrugged. "I told Astrid to collect the least sumptuous of the clothes intended for Seraphina. They ought not go to waste."

Valla stilled. She was sleeping in Seraphina's bed, wearing

Seraphina's clothes. The lines were growing blurrier by the day, and she ought to have put a stop to it long ago.

"I can't wear her clothes—sleep in her bed. It's too much."

Rodrick fixed his glacial glare on her. "You will wear what is necessary to satisfactorily attend me. If you insist on wearing those rags you drug up the mountain, you'll spend more time sick and shivering than doing your job effectively. Stop being stubborn to your own detriment."

"Very well."

Several days later, the blizzard still raged outside. She sipped at the coffee Rodrick sent her this morning, watching the wind tear at the mountainside from the queen's room. The room she could've been staying in all along—when she wasn't in Rodrick's bed, that was. White blanketed the mountain like a newborn babe. The constant howling of the wind had unsettled her at first, but now she found it peaceful—the closest thing she could get to the heady energy of a southern thunderstorm.

She was much recovered and beginning to grow bored resting in bed and tottering around her room all day.

Valla dressed in her new clothes and walked the short distance to Rodrick's door. She ignored the curious eyes of his guards and knocked.

There was a muffled "Come in."

Her mouth parted when she entered. Rodrick was shirtless, facing away from her. His loosely laced pants hung low on his hips. The muscles of his black flexed as he stretched his arms overhead in a yawn. Valla gulped.

He turned to her, flashing that brilliant smile.

"Morning, Valla. Feeling better?"

Is this what things could be like between them—*would* be like between them, if she gave it a chance? Valla shot down the thought as quickly as it surfaced. She forced her eyes away from Rodrick and knotted her hands in her skirt.

"Much. What would you have me do today?"

Rodrick combed his fingers through his short beard and thumbed his chin. "I need a shave."

She jerked her head up. "What?"

"Did you never do it in Isaana? I thought they were constantly shaving themselves to meet the sun."

"I—of course, but it's been awhile, my lord."

Of course she'd never shaved a man. She'd barely been allowed to touch a man, sequestered as she'd been. But it wasn't uncommon for wives and daughters in the south to help the men in their family shave, especially with decent mirrors being an expensive luxury.

"I never had much talent for it. Shall I fetch someone else?"

Rodrick's grin stretched. "I want you to do it. It will be good practice for my new attendant. I've already gathered everything you'll need."

Valla bit her lip. "I'll do my best."

Rodrick pulled out his low-backed desk chair and sat down. His long legs splayed out across the floor. He dwarfed the chair; he didn't sit in it so much as master it. Valla tore her eyes away from his bare chest.

She moved behind him and wet the folded towel on his desk in the waiting basin of hot water, then squeezed out the excess liquid.

"Lean your head back." In Isaana's salons they had special chairs that accommodated this pose, but they'd have to make do.

Rodrick obeyed, and she wrapped the towel around his neck and chin to soften the stiff beard hairs. His dark eyes seared into her as she settled the excess towel over his eyes.

Valla added a splash of water to his pot of shaving soap and stirred it into a thick lather with a short-bristled brush. "You want it trimmed or shaved?"

"Shaved. Isn't that how the Isaanan ladies like it, Valla?"

She blushed. In truth, she liked how his beard softened the harsh lines of his jaw. It made him slightly less devastating to look at.

"Not all Isaanan women are alike, you know."

"And what do you like? You're the only Isaanan woman I know."

"What I like isn't important. What do northern women like?"

"Beards as thick as a bear's fur."

"You'll be at a disadvantage, then."

Valla unwrapped the cooling towel from his neck and set it aside. Rodrick kept his eyes closed. The shaving cream smelled like him—pine trees and frost. Clean and wintry. Every time she caught a whiff of it on his skin, she wanted to bury her nose in his neck and inhale deep.

She scooped up a palmful of cream. He was reclined back in the chair, legs stretched out and hands crossed in his lap. A bead of water dripped into the notch at the base of his neck.

Valla tracked its path, her focus going hazy. He had a magnificent throat. Thick and muscular, with tendons that stretched beneath his skin as he tilted his head.

"Valla? I thought I was supposed to be the one lulled to sleep by this?" His voice held a hint of mirth.

She jolted out of her stupor. "Apologies. Just, uhh—analyzing the angles of your face. For the best shave."

"I thought you didn't do this often."

Valla didn't respond. She swept her hands over his jaw, working the cream into his beard. Somehow this felt more intimate than when they'd cuddled naked beneath his furs, his sizable erection pressed against her ass.

Rodrick's eyes were open now, tracing her face as she

worked. She mapped the curves of his lips with her pointer fingers, dipping into his cupid's bow. Her heart hammered in her chest.

She should have refused. This was far too familiar an action for a king and his maid. She pictured herself helping him shave before they attended a feast together, where they announced something as the king and queen of Frostheim—perhaps of all Valenmur.

Valla's finger slipped, and a dab of cream marred the plump skin of his lower lip. She leaned over Rodrick and wiped it off with the pad of her pinky finger. His lips were surprisingly soft. The pink inner line of them was visible and wet with saliva. Valla tore her hand away and quickly finished spreading the cream over the rest of his facial hair.

Rodrick had—blessedly—closed his eyes again, though he was by no means relaxed. His muscles bunched beneath his clothes, his knuckles white where his hands gripped his thighs.

"Where's your razor?"

His voice was gravelly when he answered. "Upper left drawer of my desk."

Valla rifled through map scrolls and scraps of paper until she found it. She snapped open the blade, and the edge shone wicked sharp.

Her hands shook as she hovered over his face with the naked blade. She steeled herself and lowered it to his skin, scraping it up his throat to his jawline.

She dunked the blade in the bowl of water, washing off the hair and cream, then took another swipe up the long column of his throat. The razor was sharp as sin, with an ivory guard and handle. Her first few strokes were hesitant and left short hairs behind, but once she learned the proper angle, the resulting shave was smooth and spotless.

Rodrick's throat flexed as he swallowed.

He was so vulnerable like this, letting her hold all the

power. She could plunge the blade into his neck, bleed him out. They'd probably toss her off the mountain. He might even manage to kill her before he died, but it'd be the end of the war. The end to her father's enemies. There was no heir to the winter throne. The battle for succession would distract them from their quarrels with Isaana for a while.

But then another Storm King would rise. At least Rodrick showed some capacity for gentleness. Would the frost heart die with him, or would it fly back to the heart of an ice dragon and bide its time, waiting for the next person fool enough to seek power at any cost?

When she pictured blood spilling across Rodrick's pale neck, the laughter fading from his brilliant eyes, a screw of guilt twisted through her belly. She was tired of sacrificing for her father. A man who'd given her little but her name, and she'd give that up in an instant. Had already begun the process of shedding it, like a skin that fit too tight.

"Valla? Why'd you stop?"

Why had she given him that name? One only used by people she loved. A key to the deepest parts of her. The blade shook in her hand.

Rodrick's large, warm fingers wrapped around her wrist, stilling the razor. "Careful. You'll make me bleed. And if you've a mind to, make it quick."

Valla gripped his chin and twisted his head so she could see the underside of his jaw again. She slid the razor against his skin in slow swipes.

"Are you sure you've done this before?"

Her lips twisted. Was he questioning her because of her hesitance, or had she done something wrong? She'd have to season her lies with truth. "To be honest..."

Rodrick arched an eyebrow, silver eyes sparking.

"I have no brothers, and my father discouraged me from touching men in such an intimate fashion."

Rodrick chuckled. "Touch all you like then, princess."

Valla's heart tripped in her chest. "What'd you call me?"

"Merely a nickname. For someone with hands soft as milk."

"Don't call me that."

"As you wish."

Valla returned her focus to the shave, making sure she left no hair behind. She grew accustomed to handling him freely, turning his face as she desired and pulling his skin taut to ensure she didn't nick him.

When she reached his mustache, she had to thumb his upper lip and tug it down to smooth out the skin. His hot breath ghosted across her fingers.

"I've often wondered if southern women follow the same tradition."

Valla swallowed. She'd never shaved someone's face before, but she'd shaved her legs a few times, when she was feeling particularly daring. It was common practice for the women in her father's harem to remove all their body hair—even that between their legs—though many of them preferred to use hot wax.

"You didn't have the opportunity to find out?"

"No, not many women frequenting the war camp of the enemy invader."

She raised an eyebrow at him. Sex workers in war camps were as common as flies on shit. "I find that hard to believe."

When your country was wartorn, you'd take money where you could find it.

"Ladies of the night make fine spies and assassins. I didn't let them in."

"I'm sure your warriors were thrilled with that."

Rodrick laughed. "I think it made them grateful for the frost heart's curse."

The rasp of the razor against hair was soothing. She cleaned up the edges of his sideburns.

"You didn't answer me, Valla."

Valla's core pulsed. He knew she wasn't bare. He'd seen her naked—a plentiful amount.

"It isn't uncommon for married women to remove all their body hair, even pubic."

His voice was a low rasp. "The men as well?"

Valla's cheeks warmed. Had he intended the image that sprang to her mind of her kneeling between his legs, shaving the hair at the base of his rigid shaft?

"Yes." Her voice was a squeak.

He smiled. The look in his eyes said he knew exactly what he was doing. "I'm not sure I trust you with my razor that much yet."

Valla snorted. "But you trust me at your throat?"

"Should I not?"

"I don't know."

"Such honesty. You might have thought about it a time or two, but I don't think you want to kill me."

Valla dunked the razor a final time and wiped it dry, then ran the damp towel over his face to remove any lingering hairs or cream. She was reluctant to finish; she didn't want to stop touching him. Her hand rested on his broad shoulders as she cleaned his face. There was so much latent power there, muscles coiled like a snake preparing to strike.

"Do you have any aftershave balm or serum?"

"Aye. From Isaana." Rodrick's voice was rough, his eyes heavy-lidded. His fingers fisted in his pants.

Valla identified the small bottle on his desk and squeezed a few drops into her palm with the dropper. It had a cooling sensation on the skin and would help prevent irritation.

Valla spread it on her hands and leaned over the back of the chair. She traced the pads of her fingers over the harsh jut of his jaw and the flexing cords of his throat. Then she trailed them behind his ears, across the arch of his eyebrows, and along his temples before bringing them center to absently caress his lower lip.

Rodrick wore the evidence of his responsibilities on his face and skin. But relaxed like this, she could envision what he might have looked like as a young man first coming into his power.

"Valla," he groaned.

"Close your eyes," she whispered.

He obeyed immediately, but she didn't miss the spark of lightning in his irises as his lids lowered.

She was mad. A woman possessed. She leaned forward, her breasts hanging just above his mouth.

She ached. She imagined him drawing her nipple between his lips, still covered by the fabric of her dress, and sucking until it strained against the cotton.

Her breathing quickened. What would it feel like to have him touch her? To have his big body flush against hers for a purpose beyond warmth?

She lowered her face to his and breathed in his delicious scent. She wanted to explore him, but she couldn't let this get any more out of hand than it already had.

"Don't move."

There was a spasm in his cheek, and he exhaled harshly. But Rodrick remained still.

She lowered her lips to his, pausing an inch away to share his breath. Her curls fell over his shoulders and chest. The smell of his shaving cream flooded her nose. His scent was heady, divine.

She took his lower lip between hers in the barest of kisses. She drug her teeth across his flesh in a slow tug, and Rodrick groaned. His fingers dug into the leather arms of the chair.

Emboldened, she kissed him again, opening wider for him. He tasted clean and raw.

He didn't move, remaining true to her request. Part of her regretted it—wanted him to break and fist his hands in her hair, to devour her mouth with his, to lift her against him and carry her to his bed, mere feet away.

The other part enjoyed the opportunity to explore him without risk. She liked being in control, having power over him. She had limited experience kissing, all of her trysts having been hurried affairs in hidden alcoves and dark garden paths. There'd been no slow exploration of her lovers in the sun. She wasn't allowed that privilege of youth.

Valla kissed him softly, then grew more adventurous, sucking on his lips and mouthing his skin, testing the smoothness of the shave with her tongue. Her hands wrapped around his neck, her thumbs on his jaw posing him as she liked.

Heat swirled between her thighs at the noises Rodrick made and the shudder of his muscled frame beneath her hands. He was a caged animal being denied his favorite meal.

She tightened her grip on his neck and slid her tongue along his. Frost shot down her throat as his magic surged into her. The chair legs rattled against the floor.

"Release me," he growled. Rodrick's magic began touching her where he couldn't. It raced down her throat and spine, stopping to swirl and tingle between her legs and down the inside of her thighs. Energy hummed between them everywhere they touched.

She wanted to. Wanted him to devour her with every ounce of repressed hunger evident in the muscles straining beneath her touch and the thick erection pushing against his pants. The muscles of his neck were stretched taut and pulsing. The aggressive bob of his throat as he swallowed was a work of art. She drew back and bit her lip.

Rodrick was staring at her with naked lust in his gaze. Valla's stomach dipped.

"Valla."

"I can't." If she gave in to this, she'd be gone. She would lose herself entirely to him.

His magic surged through her, caressing her nipples and clit. Like he was tracing an icecube over the most sensitive parts of her. Her knees nearly buckled.

"That's cheating."

His laugh was rich and heady. "You'll have to be more specific in your demands, princess."

She silenced him with another kiss. "Stop calling me that."

He ran a hand over his jaw, testing the shave. "You're more talented than you give yourself credit for. I'll remember this."

Fuck. Of course he would. She didn't know if she could take another session of shaving him without throwing herself at him. The temptation to settle herself in his lap and grind against him was already too much. Her body was hot and throbbing with need. Hopefully her traitorous nipples weren't visible through her dress.

She cast her eyes to the floor, sidled back, and curtsied. "Is there anything else you need, my lord?"

"I need a lot of things, Valla. But I'll take some privacy to get my hand around my cock."

Valla flushed and headed for the door. She wanted him, but that was a line they couldn't cross. She couldn't risk falling in love—or lust—with the Storm King.

His magic stayed with her this time. She could still feel it inside her, swirling through her blood like frostfire.

"Valla," he called when she reached the door.

She paused but didn't turn around. "Yes?"

"Say the word, and I'm yours."

CHAPTER 13
RODRICK

The door clicked shut behind Valla, and Rodrick scrubbed his hands over his face.

"Fuck," he grunted. He was stiff as a pike and couldn't get the feel of her soft lips out of his head. His patience and control had never been so sorely tested, but he had to let Valla take the lead. He didn't want to lose all the progress they'd made when she was finally warming up to him.

He didn't dwell on how she'd react when she learned he knew who she was. Perhaps she need never find out, and *she* could do all the confessing.

Rodrick collapsed backwards onto his bed with a sigh. He wanted to chase after her and return her kisses tenfold. He wanted to abandon this entire charade and beg her to be his.

He just *wanted*.

He wished she was his wife, wished she was warming his furs every night. Rolling over to face him in the morning with that coy grin, reaching for him under the covers to find him stiff and ready.

She surprised him more every day. The shaving had been a test—one he hadn't expected her to pass. He'd been sure she'd take the opportunity to attack him, to try and kill him. Get him out of her way for her and her father's sake. But instead she'd...enraptured him. Drug those soft hands over his skin again and again, until his blood was heated and it was all he could do not to pull her into his lap and rut against her. Wrap her around his waist and fuck her into the wall.

Even before she'd kissed him, the casual intimacy of the shave had his thoughts racing. Her careful attention to detail, her care not to cut him. She could've given him a few new facial scars, had she a mind to.

Rodrick fisted a hand over his throbbing cock. He needed to get laid, get the fiery little princess out of his system. The last problem he'd expected when going along with her ruse was sexual frustration.

It wouldn't be his first time pleasuring himself to thoughts of her. She'd left her damp panties in his room after her fall from the roof, and he'd brought himself off with them wrapped around his cock a shameful number of times. They were a simple white cotton, but imagining them flush against her tan skin, clinging to her puffy lips as she moistened them with her arousal set him off.

His cock strained against his pants with an insistent ache. Rodrick groaned and undid his laces, pulling himself out. Moisture beaded at his tip—gods, she'd really gotten him going, hadn't she? How often could he ask her to shave him without it becoming suspicious? He might have to adopt a new facial hair style.

He drew his foreskin back and pictured how she'd looked in the bath—nipples cresting the top of the water, face flush with heat. She'd tilted her heart-shaped face up to look at him with those dark eyes, hair clinging damp and humid around her face, and he was prepared to give her the world.

He spit into his palm and smoothed the moisture over his cock, then let his fantasies play out in his mind.

He pictured her returning to his bed after her bath, still dripping. Beads of water clinging to her skin, her body pink and warm. She'd crawl up his sheets, eyes dark and hungry, her damp hair grazing his skin.

She'd straddle his thighs and tease him with the wet heat between her legs before settling just below the jut of his cock.

Rodrick's cock pulsed in his hand. He wanted to feel the eager grip of her pussy as he first slid into her. To watch her eyes go wide as she took his entire length. Wanted those slick, pink walls rippling around him with each thrust.

Rodrick stroked faster, imagining the moans she'd make the first time he fucked her. The first time he stretched that tight cunt open. Her tight clutch sliding up and down his cock, coating him with her wetness, making his cock shine.

He wanted to know what Valla looked like when she came undone all over his cock. When she cried out his name and fisted her hands in his sheets.

"Fuck," he groaned as his hips began to buck. He hit his release and spurted all over his chest. He pumped himself a few more times, until come coated his hand and images of Valla eagerly licking him clean filled his head.

CHAPTER 14
VALLA

The next morning, Rodrick had Valla meet him in a small, private courtyard off their wing of the keep. It was a snow-covered clearing bordered by mountaintop. A place to feel the sun on your skin while the mountain face blocked the worst of the wind. The clearing encircled a frozen lake with a rectangular slab cut out of it.

Hundreds of ice sculptures filled the clearing. Frosted flowers, sparkling climbing vines, crystal mushrooms. A life-sized horse mid-rear, realistic except for Valla's wavy image reflecting back at her. Ice birds stuck in the sky, frozen mid-dive.

"Welcome to my ice garden," Rodrick said.

"Are—are they real?"

Rodrick sighed and shook his head. "Entirely ice. It's a hobby I took up to vent my magic. The precision and control required is good practice for me. I find it meditative."

"They're beautiful. But what are we doing here?"

"I've finally figured out what I'm going to do with you."

Her lower abdomen tightened. "You have?"

"While you're assisting me, I'm going to acquaint you

with Frostheim's customs. You've clearly many a misconception about life here, and it should help you feel like less of an outsider until spring comes."

"You don't have to do that." *Translation: I don't* want *you to do that.*

Rodrick's gaze grew flinty. "I insist."

Her eyes darted to the cutout in the lake. She was familiar with his penchant for morning ice baths—and a staunch believer that the words ice and bath did not belong together.

"You're joking."

"It's an age-old northern custom."

"You jump stark naked into a freezing pool of water. So frozen that you had to chisel a hole out of the ice."

He nodded eagerly.

"What does this have to do with me assisting you?"

"Your job as my assistant is to attend to my needs and desires. I desire that you try an ice bath."

"No."

"Yes, Valla."

"You're mad. The cold has gone to your head."

"It's refreshing. Good for your circulation. What do you think I did before coffee?"

"It's mad!" She was much warmer in her new clothes, and none too eager to part with them.

"Come, you didn't know you liked our cured salmon, either, until you tried it."

Rodrick had plied her with different creations from his cook while she convalesced, saying she needed more protein in her diet if she was going to survive winter.

"There aren't exactly a lot of options."

Cuisine in the south was far more varied. Food in the north was designed to keep you warm and energized. Flavor was a secondary consideration.

"I highly doubt Thyri took naked ice baths with you every morning. Especially several months pregnant."

"She did not."

"Then why—"

"Did your princess have to provide the rationale behind every request she made of you? You're proving to be a terrible assistant."

Valla folded her arms over her chest. "I'm not going in that water. You can't make me."

He ticked up an eyebrow that said he very well could, should he please.

"Please, Valla. Just try it. I'll go first."

Rodrick shrugged off his fur cloak and pulled the loose light blue shirt he wore over his head. Then he began unlacing his breeches with long, nimble fingers. He held her gaze as he worked, and heat crept up her neck. She'd seen it all before, but this was intentional. This was him undressing *for* her. The ice bath increased marginally in appeal.

Rodrick shrugged off his pants, kicked off his boots, then dove headfirst into the lake.

Valla gasped. What if he couldn't find the break in the ice again? The hole was small, comparatively.

Several long seconds passed. Then Rodrick surfaced in a burst of water that sprinkled her face. The water on his eyelashes crystallized immediately. His breaths fogged the air, and he let out a long, sensual sigh. The kind of sigh that belonged in a hot bath or the bedroom—definitely not a body of frigid water. He crossed his forearms on the edge of the ice and propped his chin on them. Then he lingered there, treading water.

"Are you insane? Get out! You'll freeze to death." He might bear the frost heart, but it didn't make him invulnerable to the cold, did it?

"Agree to get in."

"No!"

"We can hardly call *this* you assisting me, can we? I need you to *assist me* by getting in the water. You only need to stay in for a few seconds."

She shook her head with exaggerated force.

"By Sigurd, you're stubborn."

"I can't swim," she lied.

His brow furrowed. "Don't let go of the sides of the ice, then. If something happens, I'll dive in after you. I won't let anything happen to you, Valla."

"Please get out. You don't look so good." His lips were beginning to turn a slight shade of blue.

"You'll be getting in, then?"

She stomped her boot in the snow. "Rodrick! You insufferable man."

Clearly she needed to try a different tactic. "What will you give me if I do it?"

He barked out a laugh. "Did you bargain this much with your former mistress? I'm surprised she put up with it."

"That was different! I was never asked to do something so...unreasonable."

"What do you want me to give you?"

Valla supposed she couldn't ask him to kick Frieda off the side of the mountain. She fished for something equally unlikely.

"Chocolate. I want chocolate." Frostheim had a decided lack of sweets. The first few weeks here, her sugar cravings had been wild, but now she just longed to taste it again.

He smiled. "You got it." He pushed up on the ice with his arms, rising out of the lake with practiced ease. Drops of water ran down the muscled cords of his body, finding all his hidden valleys. His cock was flaccid with cold, but he still hung thick and long. He began toweling off with one of his furs.

Valla stared at him, aghast. "You have chocolate here?"

"I wanted the *princess* to have her usual creature comforts when she arrived."

Valla drug her toe through the snow. "Oh. How considerate."

"I'm a considerate man, Valla. Too bad she didn't have the opportunity to find out."

"Yes. Very unfortunate." At this point she would agree to jump in the water just to end this line of conversation. *Liar, liar, liar.*

She quickly stripped out of her clothes. Her nipples went taut in the cold air, and her skin pimpled with goosebumps.

She sat down on the edge of the ice with a muffled shriek.

"I'd recommend you slide in before your bits start sticking."

Valla shot him a baleful glare and braced her hands on the edge of the hole. She took a deep, fortifying breath and slid into the water.

The shock of cold surged through her, lighting up all her nerve endings. She hadn't intended to go more than neck deep, but her fingers slipped on the ice, and she went under.

Valla forced her eyes open as water slipped over her head. The muffled echoes of the lake drummed against her ears. The water was dark, the sun choked out by the thick layer of ice sealing her in. She struggled to orient herself and find the opening, then strong hands gripped her beneath the arms and pulled her up.

Rodrick smoothed her hair out of her face as the cold air pricked at her wet skin.

"You okay?"

She gave a frigid nod.

Her body's screams at her to escape the water grew muted as she slowly acclimated to the temperature.

"This isn't so bad," she said, teeth chattering. The shock

of the water reminded her a little of Rodrick's magic inside her.

Rodrick chuckled. "Aye. It's the getting in and out that's the worst part. Come on, for your first dip you shouldn't stay in too long."

He shot a beam of frost at his feet to ensure he wouldn't slide on the ice, then gripped the hand she offered him and lifted her out of the water.

The first blast of wind hit her exposed, wet flesh, freezing the water droplets on her skin.

Valla sucked in a breath. "Oh sunmother. What the fuck?" She crossed her arms and danced in place, willing warmth into her veins.

"Am I allowed to touch you today, Valla?" Rodrick's asked, his voice thick.

She nodded before allowing herself to think too much about it. Warmth took precedence over her inhibitions right now.

Rodrick pulled her to him and trailed his hands down her abdomen and hips. He tweaked one of her taut nipples and cupped her butt, pulling her into him. "Mmm. My little frost fairy."

"Now's hardly the time!"

"I beg to differ. Have you forgotten our lesson in northern survival already? Your body is so pink and soft. It makes me want to lick you all over."

Valla shuddered for an entirely different reason as heat shot to her core.

"You do this every morning?"

"Mhmm. Care to join me?" His thumbs stroked the seam between her ass and the tops of her thighs, circling dangerously close to her needy center.

"Do I have a choice?"

"You always have a choice, Valla."

He fisted a hand in her curls and tilted her head up to him. "Let me kiss you."

She shivered against him. Huddling against his breadth with his big hands cupping her ass was helping, but she wanted to crawl inside him.

"Please," she said.

Rodrick groaned and yanked her tight against him. Like she'd cut a rope gone taut and twisted. His lips met hers with a vengeance, and he devoured her mouth. He sucked on her tongue and pulled her lips between his teeth to nibble on them. He kissed like a man starved.

He gripped her thighs and lifted her off the ground without leaving her lips, wrapping her legs around him.

His heavy cock nudged against her ass, and she shimmied against it.

Rodrick let out a hoarse groan.

"Taste like my magic. Frosted strawberries and coffee."

"You left your magic in me yesterday. I can still feel it." It lingered in the pit of her stomach. Strange and unfamiliar, but welcome.

"Mhmm." He kissed along her jaw up to her ear and pulled her earlobe between his teeth.

"Why?"

"It likes you."

She moaned as he sucked at the skin between her shoulder and neck. She ground herself against his cock, wetting him with her arousal. It would be so easy for her to lift her hips and slide him inside her.

Rodrick hissed. "Fucking siren."

"We can't do this."

"We *are* doing this. But we need to stop before I lay you out on my cloak and fuck you on the ice."

Valla whimpered, and Rodrick released her. She slid down

his body, his cock dragging through the wet heat between her thighs.

He gave her a final kiss, tugging her bottom lip between his teeth as he pulled back.

He crouched to pick up his cloak from where it puddled atop his other clothes. When he turned back to her he stilled, his face going grave. The temperature dropped a few degrees, and a shiver wracked Valla.

"What is that?" Rodrick's voice was gravelly.

"What? What's wrong?" Valla followed his eyes down to where they rested on her hip.

She swallowed. The brand. This was the first time he'd gotten a good look at it. Did he know what it meant?

"You felt it the other day."

"I thought it was a scar! That design...that's intentional." Lightning sparked in his eyes, and the snow at his feet lifted and swirled in the air.

Valla's gaze fell. "It's a servant's brand."

Rodrick sank to his knees in front of her, his hot breath grazing her core. His hand reached out and traced the pattern she'd avoided looking at in the mirror for the past decade. A sun on fire—her father's insignia. Her skin pricked with cold where he touched her.

"Please tell me it's some magic, and not an actual scar..."

Valla shook her head. "It's permanent."

His snarl shook the air. One of his ice birds fell out of the sky and shattered on the lake's frozen crust.

"*Who?*"

"What?"

"Who did this to you?"

She gulped and looked away, unable to hold his gaze. "Stefan, one of the Sun King's fire mages, brands all the servants at court with his magic. He was part of the princess's entourage, so I suspect he did not survive the avalanche."

It was as close to the truth as she could tell him. She was ashamed to admit that she didn't actually *know* if the servants of the Sun Palace were branded in a similar manner, but it wouldn't surprise her. Why stop at his daughters, after all?

"Good. I hope he suffered."

She glanced back at him. The ferocity in his voice unnerved her. Why did he care so much?

Rodrick's eyes tracked hers. He rested his forehead on her hip and brushed his lips against the scar. His tenderness made her heart ache.

"Why do you want to go back there?"

Her next breath was stuttered. It was a good question—too insightful by half.

"It's where I belong."

He rose up to his full height and pushed a clump of wet hair behind her ear. His hand lingered on her, thumb rubbing her collarbone.

"Isn't belonging a place you choose?"

"It doesn't have to be *back there*. Just—"

"Not here."

She gave a stiff nod.

His fingers traced her jaw. "I'm sorry this happened to you. It makes me want to raze the fucking Sun Palace."

She chewed her kiss-bruised lip. "War isn't the answer to everything, Rodrick."

"It's the answer to this."

CHAPTER 15
VALLA

When Valla met Rodrick in the stables the next day —per the request he sent to her rooms—she was still working on her morning coffee. She'd worn the crimson cloak from her new collection of clothes, and the fabric looked like blood against the snowfall.

Rodrick glanced up from where he lounged against the stable wall and smiled. "I see I've no danger of losing you in the snow. It's a fine color on you. Drink up. We're going riding today."

"Riding?" She perked up. She loved horses and was a skilled rider.

"Sorry, I shouldn't have assumed. Do you know how to ride?"

"Of course." Valla cursed internally as soon as the words left her mouth. She'd forgotten herself—a lady's maid was unlikely to have the means to keep a horse or afford lessons.

"Perfect. We can go out on the mountain then."

When a servant led their mounts out of the stables, Valla stopped in her tracks.

Saddled before them were two tall elks with monstrous

racks twice her arm span. Velvet furred their antlers. The animals had beautiful coloring, a brown ruff over their heads and necks fading into a greyish-white over the rest of their bodies. Hooves the size of dinner plates pawed at the snow.

"You're joking, right?"

"I thought you said you rode?"

"I don't ride *that*."

"Time to learn."

Valla eyed the high stirrups. She would never be able to get into the saddle unassisted. "Could I have a horse instead?"

"The elk have surer footing in the deep snows and handle the cold better. It's not *unlike* riding a horse."

One of the elk's bellows fogged the air.

Valla stared up at Rodrick plaintively.

"I have an ancestor who's said to have trained an icebear as his mount, if you'd prefer we try that."

Valla shook her head. "Chasing bears and dragons, not to mention settling on this accursed mountain. Your family is mad."

"Yes, so much worse than the despot who brands his servants."

Valla grimaced.

"Frostheim's not so bad. You just haven't learned to appreciate her beauty yet."

"I *was* nearly buried by an avalanche on my way here."

Rodrick's lips curled into a half-smile. "I suppose that would color your perception."

He laced his fingers together for Valla to step into, then boosted her into the saddle.

He gave her mount a rough pat on the neck. "Play nice."

Valla wasn't sure if he was addressing her or the animal. She gripped the reins and tried not to think about being bucked forward onto the sharp antler tines. Still less likely to kill her than Frieda, she supposed.

"Show me the beauty, then. I'd love to be proven wrong."

Rodrick mounted with ease, sitting tall in his saddle.

"Would you, though?"

Valla's elk followed Rodrick's unprodded as he started toward the fortress gates. The shifting of the animal's gait and the shape of the custom saddle atop its tall shoulders took some getting used to. Nanook gamboled around them, digging at random patches of snow.

They were nearing the path leading up to the fiery beacon atop the mountain.

"Are we going up there?"

Rodrick nodded.

"I wouldn't have made it up the mountain without that beacon to guide me."

"The fire's never gone out. Magicked by some summer witch, no doubt." He cast her a meaningful glance. "I'm glad it was lit for you."

The beacon was farther away than it looked, and the climb to the peak was brutal. Nanook and the elks were panting by the time they crested the top of the path.

An ancient stone structure was built into the Jotunfjall's ledge. Four columns sat atop a circular slab, connecting to the stone roof above. In the center, an enormous brazier glowed hot from the fire roaring within.

Valla had felt its warmth as soon as they'd reached the peak.

They dismounted and walked to the edge of the cliff, which ended in a sheer dropoff. Valla kept a healthy distance from the edge.

Rodrick waved his hand, and the fog crowding the mountain dissipated.

"Wow."

The view from up here was breathtaking. The mountain range stretched out ahead of them in miles of rolling shadows. Even the keep looked small and insignificant from up here.

Rodrick was right—winter in Frostheim was beautiful in a fierce, sharp sort of way, much like its lord. The way a predator was beautiful right before it attacked you.

Isaana's landscapes were tame by comparison. Her home country was mostly flatland. Good for farming, but lacking in scenic vistas.

Valla drew in a deep breath of the clear, bracing air. It burned her lungs, brimming with energy and promise. Wind blew through her hair, sending her curls trailing out behind her.

Warm arms wrapped around her from behind, and she relaxed against Rodrick's chest.

Valla *liked* the Storm King. The man she could have married. The realization was odd. She'd been so prepared to hate him that liking him felt like a betrayal to herself.

"Winter becomes you. You are so much more than I ever expected."

Valla shot him a sideways glance. There were times when it felt like he was looking through her, past the disguise and the lies. Past the dirt under her fingernails and the ache in her bones to who she used to be. For she was no longer a Sunstar, but becoming something else entirely.

"Thank you. For saving me the other day. I don't think I've thanked you yet."

"Tell me if anyone continues to bother you. I don't condone that kind of behavior." Rodrick started to speak again, then paused.

"What is it?"

"Why do you really wish to return south?"

"Do I have a choice?" It was a deflection—easier than coming up with a believable answer.

"You've proven yourself worthy. There's a place for you here."

"As your servant?"

He huffed. "Is that not what you are?"

Valla's lips twisted. "Perhaps I aspire to more."

He bent his head to her ear and drew her earlobe in between his teeth, pulling until she let out a little gasp. "Perhaps I could oblige you."

Heat dropped into her belly, and she spun around to face him. "Why did you bring me up here?"

His eyes fastened on hers and held there. "The view is incredible."

"You're incorrigible."

He chuckled. "There is something else." He took her hand and led her away from the cliff's edge, toward the far side of the beacon fire.

Rodrick took the set of saddle bags off his elk and draped them over his shoulders, then strapped her mount's pack to Nanook like a harness.

"Just in case," he said. "Storms up here are unpredictable."

"Are we going somewhere?"

Rodrick began shifting snow around with his boot, exposing a stone circle inlaid with a strange symbol. He bent over and placed his hand on the carving, letting magic run through his fingertips.

Jotunfjall groaned, raising the hair on the back of Valla's neck.

Rodrick pried a rounded handle up off the stone and lifted it, opening up a dark hole in the earth.

"She was frozen shut. Been awhile since anyone's been down here."

Rodrick climbed into the hole and began to disappear beneath the earth.

"Come on," he called out.

What the fuck? Valla stepped closer and watched the top of his head descend into darkness. There were foot and hand holds carved into the side of the shaft as a rudimentary ladder.

"You've got to be kidding," she groaned.

"What are you waiting for? This can't be worse than the ice bath."

"What's down there? I can't see anything. You don't even have any light!"

"Just trust me, Valla."

She chewed her lip. He hadn't given her any reason *not* to.

"Are you at the bottom? How far is it? You better catch me if I fall."

"Of course, princess."

Valla groaned and slowly, *very slowly*, climbed down into the hole.

Something gripped her calf, and she shrieked.

"It's me. I've got you. You're at the bottom."

She couldn't see anything. She reached out for his shoulders in the dark and wrapped her arms around him, letting him pull her to the ground. "Please tell me you can magic a frost torch for us or something."

"Just a minute. Don't go anywhere." He set Valla down and moved beneath the hole once again.

Rodrick whistled once, and Nanook's head appeared over the edge of the opening, tongue lolling.

He circled his hand in the air, creating a disc of ice at the shaft's entrance.

"Come on, girl."

Nanook stepped onto the disc, and he slowly lowered it to the ground with his magic.

Valla huffed. "You couldn't do that for me?"

He shrugged. "You have thumbs."

As soon as the disc neared the ground, Nanook jumped from it and trotted off into the darkness.

"I explored these tunnels as a lad, but it's easy to get lost. The ice starts groaning and shifting, and you begin to imagine the worst. Nanook's always able to sniff the way out, though."

"What about the elk?"

"Don't worry. They know the way back to the barn, should we be late for supper. Right now they're probably napping by the fire."

Rodrick took Valla's hand and led her in the direction Nanook had vanished.

The light of the opening vanished as they went deeper. Valla clenched the back of Rodrick's shirt with her other hand. "I don't like this, Rodrick. I can't see."

"Just a minute. We're almost there."

They took a turn, and Valla saw a soft glow in the distance. As they neared it, their surroundings gradually became visible again.

They were inside a tunnel encased in ice that branched in several directions ahead of them. The ice glowed from within, almost appearing to pulse with power. The pale green color reminded her of being underwater, the sun broken and liminal through the water's surface.

Valla's jaw went slack. "What—this doesn't seem natural."

Rodrick kept walking, confident about which branch he chose to lead them down. He didn't let go of her hand, though.

"Legend has it that when the ancient ice jorumungar met his mate, he came to this mountain in search of a home for their offspring. The trickster god that lived here, atop the peak and away from the world, offered the ancient wyrm a deal. He'd leave the mountain if the jorumungar and all his descendants promised to settle here forever.

"The wyrm took the deal, and he and his mate tunneled through the rock and ice. But one day their brood exceeded the capacity of their home, and they sought to leave the mountain. They discovered their exits sealed with the magic of the trickster god. They were trapped. The bodies of the jorumungar crystallized in death, turning into the ice tunnels that give us safe passage south.

"More likely, there was once a river running through the mountain. I prefer the tales though."

Valla's ears pricked up.

"I thought the pass was the only way south? Why the fuck did we come up the mountain?"

"The presence of the tunnels is a closely held secret. It would make us vulnerable for our enemies to find out about their existence."

"So they're traversable?"

"Yes, though it's foolish to try without a guide. Too many places where the ice goes thin or slick that are indetectable to the untrained eye. And other creatures moved in when the jorumungar died."

"What sort of creatures?"

Rodrick shot her a smirk. "Let's hope we don't find out."

Valla went quiet. Why was Rodrick trusting her with this information? She could sell it to someone in Isaana for a bucket of coin, had she a mind to. Tunnels could be mapped, and Rodrick and his people would never see the attack coming.

"They're beautiful."

"Aye. Even in death."

Their voices echoed through the space, the scrape of Nanook's nails and bite of their spiked boots on ice cascading around them.

"Why trust me with this?"

Rodrick paused and turned to her. His eyes pulsed with power, their silver glow eerie in the green light of the ice. "Do you intend to betray me?"

Valla swallowed. "No."

He smiled. "Good. The elders would have my head if they knew I'd shown them to you."

They continued through the tunnels for another hour. Valla tried to keep track of the turns Rodrick took, the paths he chose, but it was impossible without a logbook or marking system. She highly doubted he was leading her south, anyways. If anything, the air got colder the deeper they went.

Eventually the tunnel narrowed, and the ice receded to darkness once again, spitting them out into a shallow cave.

A flat, endless expanse of white stretched out from the cave's entrance. Glaciers twice the size of the Sun Palace broke up the horizon. Cathedrals of ice left to sink into the sea.

Something moved in the distance, and Valla realized it was giant slabs of ice slowly crashing together atop a body of water. They creaked and groaned with each slow shift.

"Welcome to the ice flats. Known to Frostheim's loremasters as Ice Dragon's Rest."

One of the glaciers *was* suspiciously draconian. Is this where Rodrick's ancestors had stolen the frost heart, condemning its rightful keeper to this glacial graveyard?

"Can you give it back?"

"What?"

"The frost heart. Can you give it back? Give up the power."

Rodrick sighed and shook his head. "I had a great uncle who devoted most of his life to that quest, and he failed in the end. He kept diaries of his life and research. I've read them all twice over."

"Why did he want to give it up?"

"The downfall of all great men. He fell in love with the wrong woman."

Rodrick gestured to the sea of ice that stretched into the distance. "These glacial rivers are the same ones that run down the side of the mountain to irrigate Isaanan fields. They've only just begun to thaw."

They continued their trek out onto the flats. It was like walking through a portal into a strange, magical land. The blanket of snow created an unnerving silence. Like an artist had smothered all of nature's usual sounds with thick white paint. The sun reflecting off the snow was bright enough to hurt her eyes.

Valla could imagine a shadow blacking out the sky as an ice dragon returned to its nest atop a glacier. It'd land with a buffet of wings that blew up enough snow to create tiny blizzards.

Rodrick looked at home here, the silver of his eyes electric against the white backdrop. An ice lord in his natural habitat.

"As a kid, I'd come up here and go jumping across the floating slabs of ice, seeing how far out I could make it before having to turn back."

"You must have given your mother palpitations."

Rodrick's face fell.

Valla stilled, recalling that his mother had died because of the frost heart's curse.

"I'm sorry—I wasn't thinking—"

"It's okay," he said, but his eyes were far away. "You're right. She hated me sneaking away to explore the tunnels by myself."

Valla reached out for his hand and squeezed it. "She would be proud of the man you've become."

Valla had never met her own mother. The women in her father's harem weren't allowed to raise the children they bore. They were separated immediately after birth and given to a wet nurse, to be molded into her father's perfect puppets and keep the harem from vying for power.

Rodrick quickly changed the subject. "Are you cold? The wind on the flats can be brutal."

"A little," she admitted.

Rodrick shrugged out of his fur and draped it around her.

"But—"

"Don't argue. This one is already warm, and I've a spare in the saddle bags." He patted them for emphasis.

"Why are we here?"

"You'll see. But we need to wait for sunfall. I brought supplies for a fire, if we need one."

Ahead of them, Nanook began to bark and growl. Rodrick swung his head around.

"Fuck. Be quiet." He gripped her shoulder and pulled her behind him.

It took Valla a moment to spot the source of concern it. It was the black gums studded with rows of teeth that ultimately ruined the creature's camouflage.

An icebear as big as the elk she'd ridden this morning was baring its teeth at Nanook in a low growl.

Valla gasped. "Oh—"

"Shhh. Stay calm."

Nanook danced side to side, barking at the predator that could snap her in half with a swipe of its paw. The hound lunged, and the bear's roar shook the valley. Snow shuddered atop the rocks.

Valla completely froze. The hairs on the back of her neck stood on end as the bear ambled forward.

"Nanook—you have to do something, Rodrick." Her nails were biting into his skin.

She felt the familiar tingle of his power arc between their skin before it filled the air, then a tall snowbank rose out of the ground. Rodrick pulled Valla down behind it.

He whistled twice, and Nanook turned her head. The icebear moved an alarming distance in the time the hound let her attention stray.

Two more sharp whistles, and Nanook sped back toward them, kicking up snow behind her.

Valla released the breath she'd been holding when the bear didn't give chase.

Rodrick fisted his hands in the scruff of Nanook's neck and tugged her behind the snowbank.

"Stay, girl. You've no business going toe to toe with an angry icebear. I've scars enough for the both of us from the last one."

Nanook whined and sat on her haunches. Valla and Rodrick crouched behind the snowbank, peeking over the top to keep an eye on the bear.

"Don't hurt her," Valla said. "You don't need another fur."

Rodrick snorted. "I *always* need more furs, but I've no intention of harming her. Just trying to keep my girls safe."

Valla's heart fluttered.

"Watch," he said, nodding toward the bear.

The bear stared at where they'd disappeared to for several long seconds.

"What are we doing?" Valla asked in a sharp whisper. They weren't nearly far enough away for her liking—she'd never outrun the bear in this snow.

"Just wait."

After several tense minutes, the icebear relaxed and began snuffling in the snow. A white, downy head appeared by her front paw, then a second. Two fluffy cubs popped up from their den.

"Oh sunmother." She squeezed Rodrick's hand.

They watched for several minutes as the cubs chased one another between their mother's legs. They slid on their fat little bellies through the snow, tumbling into each other.

"They're adorable. I want one."

"I think you'll have to take that up with their mother."

"What should we do?"

"She'll be territorial and aggressive around her den to protect her cubs. I think there are some caves near here. We can settle in and wait her out. With any luck, she'll go out hunting or settle in for a nap. It's about time for lunch anyways."

CHAPTER 16
VALLA

The cave Rodrick found was surprisingly cozy. He built them a fire and walled off the entrance with a thick layer of ice, which kept the warmth in and the icebears out.

They lunched on strips of cured meat and cheese and passed the dragon's milk in his flask back and forth. Nanook was curled up by the entrance, snoring softly.

"And here I thought you said these supplies were for emergencies."

"I packed plenty. Eat."

"Uh huh. Sure you didn't plan for an encounter with a dangerous animal followed by a romantic meal in a cave? It reads like one of my sister's novels."

"Romantic, is it?"

Valla groaned and took another sip of the dragon's milk.

"I don't often have the opportunity to get away from the keep. Not for pleasurable pursuits, anyhow.

"And is this? A pleasurable pursuit?"

"That's up to you, Valla."

Her cheeks heated. She averted her gaze and tore another strip of meat off with her teeth.

"It's been too long since I've come out here. Away from it all. The untamed energy of this place makes matters of state seem insignificant.

Valla nodded. "It feels otherworldly."

Rodrick sat with his back propped against the wall of the cave, knees bent in front of him.

"Come here," he said, parting his knees and patting the space between his thighs. Those electric grey eyes were heavy on her, lingering.

Valla chewed her lip. Here, they weren't the Storm King and the Sunstar or Rodrick and the lady's maid. Here they were just a man and a woman, alone in a cave on top of the world.

Valla crawled over to him, passing him the flask and situating herself between his legs. Her back was stiff as a board.

"Relax," he said, stroking one of her curls. "I'm not going to hurt you."

Valla leaned back against his chest. His arms wrapped around her middle, and he stroked his thumb down her stomach. He was so big and warm, surrounding her like this. She was hyper aware of everywhere their bodies touched.

Valla needed a distraction from the tension building between them. "Tell me about your great-uncle. The one who tried to rid himself of the frost heart after falling in love with the wrong woman."

Rodrick sighed. "It's a sad story."

"All northern stories are sad."

He chuffed softly, hot breath blowing across her neck. "Comes with the perpetual cold and darkness, I'm afraid."

"Tell me. Please."

"Alright, princess. My great-uncle Riggan inherited the

frost heart along with his brother—and my great-grandfather —the king. Great-grandpa already had several children securing the line of succession. So, as is the wont of second sons, Riggan longed for adventure. But Riggan could only explore the world two weeks at a time—one week there, one week back—before the curse's leash began to choke. Constrained by this distance, he made thorough exploration of the Isaanan peninsula. There he met an Isaanan girl, Rachel, with hair black as a winter night and eyes like a hearthfire banked low."

"Bit poetic, was he?"

Rodrick chuckled. "Aye. Another curse of his. He and Rachel fell in love and lived together in the south. But again and again, he had to leave her. Finally, she confronted him about his absence, and he told her the secret of our cursed bloodline. He asked her to come north with him, so he'd never have to leave her again.

They built a small house on the border of Frostheim and Isaana, but soon Rachel longed for the comforts of home. Every month, she took a trip to see her family and soak up the sun. And every month, it was longer before she returned."

"Ugh. This is going to end depressingly, isn't it?"

"Would you like to change the ending?"

Valla waved her hand. "Get on with it."

"Rachel begged him for a child, but he wouldn't give her one, afraid to pass on the curse. Riggan buried himself in texts on magic, teaching himself long-dead runic languages so he could decipher ancient scrolls. He hunted for a flame dragon's heart, hoping it might counteract the curse, even though the dragons had been gone for hundreds of years. He grew obsessive, desperate.

"One day, Rachel didn't return home from her trip south. Riggan waited each day to see her cresting the top of their valley. The worst blizzard of an age raged all month long—in the middle of summer, mind you. Crops for miles were ruined, and the valley was buried shoulder-deep in snow. When a full month passed and still she didn't return, Riggan went searching for her.

"He found her at home with her family. She hadn't run from him. Hadn't been kept by force, forbidden to return. Rachel told him she'd return with him if he agreed to give her a child—just one, though she'd longed for a large family like her own. But Riggan wouldn't compromise. Said he wouldn't risk condemning their children to the half-life he was cursed with."

"Stubborn git. Doesn't sound like half a life to me."

Rodrick's hand absently stroked through her hair.

"Riggan abandoned their valley home and returned to Frostheim. He ceased his exploring. He wrote Rachel letters he never sent for the rest of his life, and she married an Isaanan and had many children.

"Riggan's last letter to her said, *'It wasn't until I lost you that I truly knew the meaning of living half a life. Because without you, I lost the other half of my soul.'*"

Valla swiped at the tear leaking down her cheek. "I hate this story. Did they ever get to see each other again?"

"He tried. Once he grew grey enough to realize he didn't have many trips down Jotunfjall's back left in him, he went south a final time—the first time since he'd left her, all those years ago. He brought the stack of unsent letters, hoping they might laugh and reminisce over young love lost. That he might stir her heart to give him one last chance.

"A woman who looked just like Rachel, same as the day he'd met her, answered the door. Sent him back in time for a moment. It was her oldest daughter. Rachel had died five years before. Uncle Riggan did not live long after that. He was buried beside her, in the field where they met."

"Sunmother, northern stories are all so morose. And your great-uncle was a fool."

"How would the tale end in the south, then?"

"The same, likely, but the point of it would be different."

"Oh?"

"If it was an Isaanan harem wet nurse telling this tale, it'd be all about how the grass isn't actually greener on the other side. In fact, there's *no* sodding grass on the other side, nor is there chocolate or coffee or sunlight or warmth. And a good southern lass should've had more sense than to go trying to thaw the heart of an ice lord."

Rodrick chuckled. "Ah, that does sound familiar. Though ours is all about how southern lasses burn bright, but the brighter the flame, the quicker it's quenched. Not like a good steady northern lass, who will burn slow and steady and birth you many strapping children."

Valla snorted. "Very compelling."

"For what it's worth, I agree with you. Great-Uncle Riggan was a fool. But perhaps I can learn from his lesson."

She stilled. What did he mean by *that*? The slow stroke of his fingers and the warm embrace of his body had stoked a fire in her, simmering low and ready.

She wanted to banish the bitter promise of his tale and her inevitable return south.

Release me, he'd told her the first time she kissed him. She wanted him to break. To unleash all that raw power he kept caged on her.

Valla knew him well enough now to know he wouldn't make the first move. Not when, to his knowledge, the balance of power between them was so skewed.

She was already puzzled by his behavior. This felt more like an outing one would make with a friend, a lover, than with a personal attendant. He was sharing his favorite parts of the north with her—*eager* for her to like it, or at least appreciate it. *Were* they friends? Something more?

The idea was ludicrous.

"Rodrick."

He looked up from the fire. "Hmm?"

Valla swallowed. She'd never so boldly come onto a man before.

"I've a better idea for how we might pass the time than sad tales."

His body tensed behind her, then his voice became a quiet purr in her ear. "Do you now?"

She let her head fall back against his shoulder and brought her lips to his neck. "I want you."

Rodrick swallowed, the cords of his throat bobbing beneath her lips.

The silence stretched long, and Valla began to second guess herself. What was she thinking? She was no one to him. An amusement. A dalliance. She pulled away, steeling herself for his rejection.

Rodrick gripped her jaw and tugged her face around towards him. Lightning danced in his slate colored eyes.

"Are you certain, Valla? Are you sure this is what you want?"

She could feel how tense he was against her.

In answer, she stood up and undid the clasp of her cloak, letting it puddle to the floor around her. She turned, presenting the long row of buttons down the back of her dress, and twisted her head over her shoulder to look at him.

That was all the permission Rodrick needed. He was on his feet in a second, striding toward her and spinning her into his arms. He captured her mouth in a fierce kiss, wrapping his hand in her curls and pulling her roughly against him.

He lapped at her, letting his magic flow freely between them. It wrapped around her and shot to all her sensitive places, setting them tingling.

His nimble fingers made quick work of her buttons.

"The only reason I'm not ripping this dress off you is because I don't want you to suffer the cold later."

"How considerate of you." Her breath was ragged.

"I'm a considerate man."

"Show me how considerate you can be."

Rodrick slid the dress down her shoulders, baring her body. Valla's nipples pebbled in the cold, goosebumps prickling her skin.

His eyes traced the curves of her body, and he inhaled deep.

"Bloody gorgeous."

"Touch me. I'm cold."

Rodrick wrapped his hands around her middle and stroked his thumbs up and down her ribs. His head fell to her neck, lips mouthing at her shoulder as his hands trailed down her body.

Rodrick pulled back, and she whimpered in protest at the loss of his heat.

He pulled a spare fur from his saddlebags and spread it out on the ground.

Valla slid her underwear down her hips and stepped out of them. She wanted all of him tonight, while she could still have him, in this stolen moment on top of the world. They were miles away from anyone who would care, who could judge what was about to happen between them in this cave.

"Lay down," he said, voice gruff.

Valla lowered herself to the furs and stretched out on her back. She bent her knees and spread her legs for him.

The air crackled with magic. "Goddess, I don't deserve you."

Rodrick dropped to the fur and covered her body with his. He scraped his teeth down the line of her jaw. Then his mouth was at her neck, where he bit her hard enough to bruise and lapped over the spot with his tongue.

Valla ran a hand through his thick hair and clutched his muscled back. He left a magical imprint everywhere he touched. A frosty tingle, an erotic ache.

He squeezed her nipples until she squeaked. It was pain and pleasure, push and pull. She was water in his hands, and he a master of manipulation.

Rodrick kissed his way down her sternum to her navel, pausing to swirl his tongue inside the scoop of flesh before moving lower still. He buried his nose in her curls and inhaled.

"Rodrick—"

"Shh. Let me give you this." His fingers traced the seam of her pussy. "I've wanted to touch you here for weeks. To feel how wet you get for me."

He cupped her behind the knee and lifted her leg over his shoulder, parting her dusky petals for him.

"Mmm. Is all this for me? What a good girl."

He swiped his tongue up her slit, and Valla's hips jerked.

He toyed her swollen clit with his tongue, then spread her apart with his fingers.

"So wet for me, princess."

She didn't protest the nickname. Valla let herself pretend she wasn't lying to him—that he knew the whole truth of her and wanted her anyways.

Rodrick laved her core again, and Valla shuddered, fisting her hands in his hair. He traced her opening with a finger, spreading her slickness before sinking inside her to his third knuckle. Valla gasped and rolled her hips into his face.

"Yes, baby. Show me how you like it."

He ate her like his last meal on earth. She was swollen and hot and aching. He added a second finger, stretching her taut around him.

"You're gonna be so tight when I split you open on my cock."

His crude words sent desire zipping through her.

"I can feel you clench around me when I speak. Do you like when I talk dirty for you? You like filthy words about this pretty pink cunt and all the depraved things I want to do to it?"

Valla nodded fervently.

His fingers curved up inside of her, stroking a spot that made her lower abdomen tighten. Then he attacked her clit with his tongue.

"Rodrick! Fuck!"

Her hips writhed beneath him, but he forced her legs to stay spread, pinning her open.

"Come for me, princess. Come all over my face. Let me taste you."

He quickened his ministrations, fingers moving faster, pressing deeper.

She clenched around him as fire seized her body, quivering as she rode out the sensation.

"Beautiful."

She continued to quake beneath him for several long seconds, her belly undulating with the force of her breaths.

Rodrick sat up and stripped off his shirt, exposing taut muscles shaped by battle.

Valla unlaced his pants with eager fingers and pulled his cock out. He was bigger than she'd ever seen him, swollen and straining. Precum dribbled from the head of his cock.

She stroked him from root to tip.

Rodrick groaned. "Fuck. Careful."

He scrambled out of his pants and blanketed her naked body with his. He was all raw, male power. Strung tight and eager to break free,

His straining cock bobbed against her belly, painting her with precum. They both groaned as he rocked his shaft between her wet folds.

"Inside me."

Lightning sparked in his eyes. "Yeah? You want me to fill you up? Stretch you out?"

His cock slid against her oversensitized clit, and she strained against him.

"Please," she whimpered.

Rodrick nocked the head of his cock against her entrance and began to slide in.

Valla threw her head back. He was larger than she'd ever taken before.

"Fuck. So tight, princess." He fed her inch after inch, slowly stretching her out on him. When he finally sank balls deep, he paused there, breathing hard and letting her adjust to the fullness.

Her hands stroked down his back to his ass. She arched her back and swirled her hips, urging him to move.

Vibrant eyes met hers. He pulled out and thrust his entire length back in, fast and hard and full.

"Is this what you want, Valla? Every inch of my cock? Fucking you so hard you can't think?"

She groaned when he bottomed out. He was big enough to bump against her cervix.

Rodrick slid out again. He kept the head of his cock at her entrance, teasing her with it.

"Rodrick!"

"Say it."

She felt so empty. She needed him deep inside her again, filling her up. "Fuck me, Rodrick. Please. I need—"

Rodrick buried himself inside her. He leaned over her, hands bracketing her head as he dipped into her, over and over. His ass flexed taut as he chased his pleasure with each thrust.

It was a brutal pounding. An aching thud of pleasure every time he thrust his full length into her. His eyes were fixed on hers, and it was difficult to hold his gaze. She felt exposed. Like he could see all her secrets shifting beneath her skin.

"You're taking me so well."

Valla clenched around him. His magic pulsed across their skin. She bent her legs in the air, and he slid even deeper, the angle of his next pump more intense.

Rodrick hissed and gripped the back of her thighs, keeping her spread open for him, pinned on his cock.

His magic concentrated on her clit, mimicking the quick stroke of his fingers.

"Fuck!" she cried out. Valla raked her nails down his back as pleasure surged down her spine. She tightened around him, and Rodrick released a ragged groan.

"Feel so good. Gonna come all over my cock?" He reached a hand between them and slid his thumb over her clit, stroking hard and fast, sending her spiraling—

Rodrick captured her mouth with his as she went over the edge. The cords of his neck flexed. His hips strained against her as his cock kicked inside her, shooting deep. Her walls fluttered around him, and he bit her lip hard enough to bruise as groans of praise spilled from his lips.

Rodrick collapsed on top of her, then rolled them over so Valla rested atop his chest. Her pussy spasmed around him as her orgasm faded, and his cock pulsed in response.

She could feel his cum leaking out around where they were still joined. Valla burrowed into his chest and breathed deep on his scent.

Rodrick stroked his hand through her hair, then down her back, over and over again, until sleep claimed her.

CHAPTER 17

VALLA

"Wake up, Valla."

Valla rolled over into Rodrick's chest. "Hmm? It's still dark out."

"So it is."

"Tired," she mumbled.

"It'll be worth it. You'll see."

Rodrick stood and offered her his hand, and she let him pull her up. He bundled her up in furs and gave her a searing kiss.

Rather than melting the ice filling the cave's entrance, he carved a hinged door into it with his magic. He opened it and stepped through, bowing with a flourish.

"My lady."

She snorted. "Showoff."

Valla stepped out and took a deep breath of the cold, bracing air. Inside the cave's warmth, wrapped up in each other, she felt like nothing could harm them, but out here, reality was coming crashing back in.

Her train of thought was cut off when Rodrick put a finger under her chin and tilted her head up.

Valla's breath escaped her. Fiery ribbons of light illuminated the sky. Waves of green, purple, and blue danced among the stars. The undulating colors lit up the horizon as far as she could see. They crawled through the sky, resonating to a celestial tune.

"What are they?"

Rodrick shrugged. "Paintings by the gods. Strange magic from a time giants walked the land. Weather phenomena. No one really knows."

She thought he'd wanted to show her the stars, but the reality was so much better.

"They're beautiful."

Valla glanced up at Rodrick when she felt his gaze lingering on her. He was staring at her intently.

"You're not even looking," she said.

"I've something far more beautiful in my sights."

She fought back a smile. "Careful, sir, or I'll begin to question your taste."

"I have impeccable taste."

"That's why one of your favorite foods is pickled herring?"

"Not my favorite. That'd have to be coffee, lately."

"If it's not your favorite, then why do they serve it four times a week?"

"It's plentiful and lasts all winter long."

Valla shuddered. "Can't wait to get off this mountain."

She'd meant it playfully, but the way his face instantly fell made her heart ache. She would miss Rodrick when she returned south. She no longer had any doubts about that.

His expression closed off, and he looked out into the distance, to where the ice careened together in the surf.

"Do you hate it here so much?"

Valla hesitated. She was surprised to realize she didn't. If anything, her time in the north was proving to be one of the adventures she'd always craved. A chance at independence. Frostheim was slowly growing on her—much like its master.

"No. There is beauty to be found here, amongst the snow and ice. More than I expected."

"But not enough." His voice was bitter.

Valla swallowed. It was cruel to continue to lie to him. To let him believe he and his home weren't enough, when it was so much bigger than that.

"Is there anything that could make you stay?"

Valla crossed her arms and knotted her fingers together in her fur wrap. "I don't know."

"I thought showing you the beautiful things we have to offer may change your mind. I see I was wrong."

Valla's heart kicked. She fell back on her lie—one final time, she told herself—and tried to pull them back to the serenity of a moment ago. "Don't be maudlin. You're a king. I'm a servant. Nothing permanent can come of this."

His lips tightened. "Right."

"Thank you for bringing me out here. For showing me the things that are special to you. I wish I could do the same."

"Why can't you?"

"You're familiar with your great-uncle's tale. How would ours end any differently?"

Rodrick shook his head and strode back toward the cave. "Look your fill. Don't stray far."

He whistled and pointed, and Nanook settled on her haunches at Valla's feet, standing guard.

Valla's guilt gnawed at her stomach. She wanted to tell him the truth—she really did—but what if he didn't let her leave? He would always choose the good of his people before her. And if he tried to keep her here, it would ruin all they'd shared. She was through with gilded cages.

Their ending was an inevitability.

· · ·

WHEN VALLA RETURNED to the cave, Rodrick was staring into the fire, face tense.

"We're staying here tonight?"

"It's much colder out there without the sun, and snowcats stalk the night."

Valla drug her toe against the floor, scraping up a fine layer of powdered ice.

"Won't people wonder where you are?"

"I told Astrid to make my excuses if we were late getting back."

"The elk will return on their own?"

"Aye. And if they didn't show for supper, Franz will have gone looking for them."

"Good. That's good."

They stared at each other in an uncomfortable standoff, the air between them thick with things unsaid.

She couldn't be falling for him. The idea was ridiculous. He was *him* and she was her and he had no idea who she was, just some servant that he treated like royalty—but perhaps this was how he was with all women?

"I don't want things to be awkward between us," she said.

"Perhaps we should fuck again."

She huffed out a laugh. "You think that the best solution?"

"I think it'd distract you from the awkwardness."

"Temporarily."

"We'll just have to keep distracting you then, won't we?"

Valla knelt beside him, her body already heating at the thought of lying with him again. "We have to stop, when we return."

Rodrick's lips tightened. "If you say so."

They didn't remove any clothes. Rodrick hiked her dress over her waist, freed his cock, and slid inside her ready wetness.

Any gentleness of their first coupling was gone. He took her hard and fast, directing her body as he liked. He bent her over onto all fours and slammed into her from behind, thrusting into her with fierce grunts, pulling her hair so her back arched as he spilled inside her.

Afterwards, they curled up together atop his cloak, a fur wrapped around them.

When the fire had long burned down to embers, Valla still stirred, her thoughts racing.

She thought she'd be able to keep sex and her feelings for Rodrick separate, but they were already braiding themselves around each other, as sure as his hot palm against her abdomen and his breath ghosting her neck.

The wetness seeping between her thighs was an uncomfortable reminder that they'd had unprotected sex twice now. It was foolish—something she'd never dared risk in Isaana, where she'd taken a regular contraceptive tea during her few dalliances.

She couldn't get pregnant; she had to leave. And Rodrick still didn't know her true identity. She ought to tell him, here in this cave. Before they slept together again. Before she let this go any further.

"I can hear your thoughts churning. What's wrong?"

She shrugged. "Not used to sleeping in ice caves."

"Be honest with me for once, Valla."

"You finished inside me, and I didn't stop you. Didn't *want* to stop you. What if I conceive?"

His hand curved around the bump of her lower abdomen. "We can get you a contraceptive tea, should you wish. Ask Astrid when we return to the keep."

Should she wish? Wasn't he worried about conceiving a bastard with his late fiancée's servant?

"You don't seem concerned."

"I'm not."

"But—"

"I already told you, Valla. I want you to stay. You're the one determined to leave."

"But a child—"

"Would be cherished."

He was mad. Any child out of wedlock would complicate the succession, let alone a child with an Isaanan.

The boundaries of her own identity were growing blurrier in her mind. She was so tired of playing pretend. But who did she want to be, at the end of this? She could leave the Sunstar name behind for good, become Valla the lady's maid in truth, with a million possibilities before her. She could be anything, but could she be his?

Rodrick's erection pushed against her spine, and he nipped at the back of her neck. "Do I need to distract you again?"

"Is that all this is for you? A distraction?"

He ran his tongue up the edge of her ear. "No, Valla."

"This is madness."

"This is everything."

CHAPTER 18

RODRICK

Rodrick slid his arm around Valla's hip and pushed his palm into her lower belly, right above her pubic mound. His hands looked huge on her petite frame.

It'd been foolish, to spill inside her. But the hot clutch of her pussy around him had been so sweet, and the instinct to fill her with seed was strong. She was his, godsdamnit, and he wanted to mark her. Fill her. Watch her belly grow.

A child would be a permanent tie between them. He didn't want to trap her, but he was already unable to picture a future where she wasn't *his*. He would convince her to stay. Somehow. She belonged beneath his furs, wearing his ring.

He cut the thought off there. If he was smart, he'd begin distancing himself from her. Valla was going to leave, and she wouldn't be coming back. Not even for him.

So instead, he sought the familiar oblivion of sex.

Rodrick slipped his fingers through Valla's curls and cupped her between the legs.

He took his straining cock in hand and slid it between her thighs, stroking slowly back and forth, parting her lips and spreading the mix of slick and spend. He rubbed her clit until she was grinding back against him.

"The feel of our come wetting my cock drives me crazy. Such a messy pussy."

Rodrick twisted and pulled at her nipples with each hump against her little slit. The head of his cock teased her entrance with each thrust.

It was torture. His cock was coated in her, slipping through her folds. He ached to bury himself inside her, but he wanted to make her beg for it first. Needed her to admit how badly she wanted this.

"Rodrick," Valla whined, her body squirming against him as she sought his cock.

He kissed the crook of her neck. "So nice and wet. You're dripping. Is that pussy ready for me, princess?"

She arched her back and ground against his length in response.

"I shouldn't have spilled inside you," he confessed. "But I couldn't bear to leave that hot clutch. And now I can't stand the thought of coming anywhere else."

She smelled like him, was full of his spend, and it sent him to a dark, primal place. He wanted to possess her.

Valla moaned.

Rodrick scraped his teeth down her neck. She would be covered in his marks.

Was he manipulating her? She was absolutely cock-drunk, but he'd ensure she received the contraceptive. It would be her choice.

"What do you say, Valla? Do you want me to give you my seed again? Do you want to feel me shooting inside you as you clench around my cock and milk out every drop?

"Gods yes."

Satisfaction swelled through him. She was writhing against him now, chasing her pleasure. After having her twice, he had the endurance to draw this out and tease her into a state of madness.

"Tell me what you want, princess."

"Inside. I want you inside me."

He pulled her leg back over his hip, and this time when he slipped through her folds, he slid the pulsing head of his cock inside her grasping pussy and bottomed out.

"Fuck," he hissed.

Valla let loose those little groans she made when she was adjusting to his size. His entry was made easier by his come filling her from earlier, but he still stretched her wide.

Rodrick kissed behind her ear and down her nape as he began to pump his hips.

"So good and tight and wet for me, princess."

He loved having her spread wide atop his cock, taking command of her pleasure as they moved in a slick glide of skin.

"So big," she panted.

"Yeah? You like me stretching you open like this?"

"Mhmm."

He paused and circled his fingers around her clit, not directly touching it.

She whined.

"Tell me what you want, Valla."

"Touch me. I need you to make me come."

He bit down on her shoulder and began moving faster, giving her long, delicious strokes as he massaged her clit.

Her whole body seized, her walls pulsing around him as she came undone.

Rodrick grunted hard. "Yes. Just like that."

Then he rolled her over, and she was belly-down on the furs. Rodrick was still inside her, his body blanketing hers. His cock slipped even deeper as he pressed down, and she keened.

"Fuck. This pussy is going to ruin me."

He had her pinned like an animal. Valla fisted her hands in the furs and writhed on his cock.

He squeezed the globes of her ass and spread them apart so he could watch his cock disappear inside her, over and over again. Her little lips stretched thin around him, his cock shining with her slick.

The sight nearly undid him. *Fuck.*

"You're gonna make me come."

Valla arched her back, lifting her ass for him, and the tip of his cock massaged her cervix.

He wanted to bruise her, ruin her, claim her, mark her—never as her father did, no, but with his teeth and cum and furs. Everyone would know she was his, even if she wasn't ready to admit it to herself.

He made to pull out, and she moaned in protest, sliding back against his pelvis.

"Valla—baby—"

"No. Come inside me," she moaned. "I want it."

He groaned. "Fuck."

He pictured his spend dripping out of her pretty pink slit, labia tinged red from his attentions, and his balls tightened even further. She'd look so pretty, swelling with their child.

"You want my cum? It's yours. All yours. Every drop."

She worked herself up and down his shaft, her breaths coming heavy. Her walls began to ripple around him, and that sent Rodrick over the edge.

He flexed his hips against her ass until his balls crowded against her. They were drawn up and tight, ready to pump her full.

He twisted her head to the side by the hair and took her mouth in a searing kiss as he began to spill inside her with slow, delicious pulses. Her little cunt was squeezing him so tight he couldn't think. His hips thrust against her mindlessly, cock pushing out his load over and over again.

"Valla—fuck."

Their heavy breaths filled the quiet air, and Rodrick collapsed against her back, bracing a shaky arm on the floor to keep most of his weight off her.

The thought of her leaving filled him with dread. He could stay like this forever.

CHAPTER 19
VALLA

They fucked twice more before their return to the keep. Once in the cave, and again against a column by the beacon fire. It was a frenzied, hurried coupling, like they both knew the magic of the ice flats was fading. That things couldn't stay this way for long.

Rodrick filled her with his cum each time, and Valla didn't stop him—encouraged him, even. The way he lost control as he neared release was addictive, and she planned to take the contraceptive tea as soon as they returned.

"We have to stop when we get back," she'd panted against his neck, her legs hitched up around his waist as he thrust into her.

"If you say so, princess."

She'd stopped objecting to the use of the nickname altogether, falling further into her delusion.

As soon as they returned to the keep, Valla sought Astrid out in the practice yard. She was in the middle of running drills with her recruits.

"Astrid, can I speak with you?"

The shieldmaiden swiped the sweat off her brow and motioned for her troops to continue.

"What's up? How was your trip to the flats?"

Valla paused, struck by irrational jealousy. Did Rodrick take all his women there? Had he and Astrid once been a thing?

Astrid sensed the change in mood and smirked. "He mentioned that's where he was taking you. He's tried to show me, but I can't stand being cooped up in those tunnels. Creeps me out."

Valla mustered a smile. She had no business being jealous when she wasn't planning on sticking around.

"Do you happen to keep herbs for a contraceptive tea on hand? I—I find myself in need of some."

Astrid's brows shot up, then she broke into a grin. "Who's the lucky lad?"

Valla chewed on her lip. Astrid knew she and Rodrick had been alone in the wilderness overnight together. The implication was obvious. Still, she wasn't ready to confirm it.

"I'd rather not say."

Astrid leveled her with a knowing look. "We have the herbs. Unfortunately, Frieda controls the stores. We track our stock of medicinal herbs like that to ensure they'll last all winter, and she controls their dispensation. They're kept under lock and key. Afraid you'll have to ask her."

"Shit. Alright."

"Are you...going to continue to see him? Out of curiosity."

"I shouldn't."

Astrid chuckled. "Life's short. You should take your pleasure where you can."

She gave her a short nod. "Thank you, Astrid."

Valla swallowed her pride and sought out Frieda in the kitchens, convincing herself that asking the hearthkeeper for help was better than an unplanned pregnancy with a man she'd been lying to since the beginning of their relationship.

Surprisingly, Frieda didn't fight Valla on the matter. She even gave her a cluster of sachets for the rest of the month. Valla chalked it up to whatever Rodrick had said to her following the icicle incident.

SHE AND RODRICK did not stop.

Morning coffee led to ice baths and frenzied kisses in the cold, until Rodrick was backing her up towards his bed and nudging open her thighs, kneeling at his bedside to eat her out until her legs were shaking.

A hot bath together turned into her riding him in the tub, his hands easing her hips up and down his cock as water spilled out over the edge and he mouthed hushed praise against the slick of her neck.

The man fucked like an animal. He insisted on wringing multiple orgasms out of her before finally spending inside her, as he was only too happy to do when she told him she'd begun the contraceptive.

Valla could feel the knot between them tightening. Every time he made her come apart beneath him, every time she tried to return to her rooms at night after they made love and he pulled her back beneath his furs, wrapping himself around her until she drifted off in his arms. She'd ended up sleeping in Rodrick's bed every night since their trip to the flats.

Valla couldn't deny the perverse, primitive pleasure she got from them fucking like man and wife. Her guilt over her lie grew, but in some ways, confessing now felt even riskier than before. Rodrick's touch was possessive, and she had little doubt he'd keep her here if he knew how much claim to her he already had.

Lying naked and twined together in bed, heartbeat to heartbeat, it was easy to forget that he didn't really know the truth of her. Would he hate her, once he learned she was the daughter of his enemy? Could he ever love her without reservation, knowing her father's blood ran through her veins?

Her middle sister, Evangeline, would tell her she was behaving like one of those desert birds that stuck its head in the sand when danger neared.

Gossip in the keep following their return was out of control. Apparently Rodrick had never shown a woman such favor before, and his subjects found his behavior intriguing. Rodrick taking her on as his attendant had been the kindling, and their long, overnight absence the spark that set wagging tongues afire.

Valla avoided their lingering stares and hushed conversations by spending her time exploring Rodrick's spaces. She discovered him piece by piece. What he liked to read, the curves of his handwriting, the meticulously rendered carvings in his ice garden.

Today he'd left early to go on a hunting trip with some of his warriors, and Valla was reading in his office.

The broken window had yet to be repaired—replacement glass would likely have to be brought in from the south—but Rodrick had filled the hole with a thick layer of ice that kept out the cold.

Valla's guilt was becoming a heavy stone in her gut that refused to fade. She had to tell him—*needed* to tell him. It was eating her up inside like a wormy apple. He deserved to know the truth.

As a girl, when her guilt over some slight against her sisters had gotten the better of her and she hadn't the courage to confess to their faces, Valla would write out her sins—her confession—in a letter, slip it under their door, then run away and hide while they read it. It was immature, but to her mind, better than never confessing at all.

Evening was sinking in, the light breaking through the frost fading to a dull glow. Valla bit her lip and traced her fingers against the ice. The familiar hum of Rodrick's magic sung through her. She stood up and went to his desk, then began digging through the drawers for a piece of parchment and quill.

Her hands stilled when she turned over a letter bearing her father's seal. The same burning sun that scarred her hip.

Valla glanced toward the closed office door. Rodrick could be back any minute. Had her father responded to the news that his daughter was dead? Had he offered one of her sisters up in her stead, or would war return come spring?

Valla picked up the letter and unfolded it.

Instantly, the world began to close in around her. Her ears rang. The taste of blood filled her mouth.

She clutched the side of the desk to keep from sinking to the floor.

Her own face stared up at her from the parchment. The portrait she'd sat for with the court artist prior to her engagement.

Had Rodrick seen it?

Of course he'd seen it. It was unsealed, in his desk drawer amongst his other correspondence. He personally read them all. She'd sat and watched him flick open the wax seals with the tip of his dagger in the evenings.

How long had he known?

Valla jerked the drawer out and emptied it atop his desk. She rifled through the pile until she found more parchment bearing the Sun King's insignia. They were the terms of the treaty between their kingdoms, dated a month prior to her arrival in Frostheim.

Valla's hands shook. The pit of her stomach was a yawning hollow stretching wider and wider.

It was all a lie. *Everything*. Smoke and mirrors, two people playing pretend. Both stuck in the tangled web they'd spun about themselves.

That was how he found her, of course.

She hadn't heard the door open, but she felt the weight of his gaze on her, the faint crackle of his magic in the air.

Valla couldn't bear to look at him.

Rodrick stepped through the doorway and softly closed the door behind him.

Valla picked up the portrait. The paper shook in her hands.

"Did you see this letter?"

It was a stupid, naive question. The lies were toppling around her like a house of cards. He'd given her Seraphina's rooms and clothes, called her princess, risked bloody *pregnancy* with her.

Sunmother, she was a fool.

Rodrick slowly nodded.

She looked up, blinking tears away.

"How long?" Her voice was ragged.

"Valla—"

"*HOW LONG?*"

Rodrick wore a tortured expression. His eyes were shadowed, his magic still.

"Since the beginning."

Valla's mind was shutting down. She wanted to scream. All of this—for *nothing*.

He never intended to let her leave come spring. She was his plaything. Frieda's *dog*. She'd been a fool to seek happiness here.

How many people in the keep knew? Everyone? Were they all secretly laughing behind her back as she scrubbed on her hands and knees for the enemy? Slept in his bed and fetched him drinks? How long had he planned to let this go on?

Rodrick moved toward her. "Let me explain. This doesn't change anything."

It changed *everything*.

He reached for her, and she backed away.

Valla crumpled the drawing in her fist.

She was a fool, and Rodrick was the monster she'd always believed him to be. Her mind spun from fact to fact, lie to lie.

Her next breath was a halting sob.

"All this time?" She didn't want to believe it.

"A lady's maid would never mistake that seat for her own, Sunstar." His arms were open, hands held out like he was calming a spooked horse. Or preparing to catch her when she bolted.

"Don't call me that!"

"Valla—"

"You know that is not my name."

"Yes, it is. It's the name you chose for yourself. You are more than your station. You've made it clear that you will be whoever you wish to be, not what others would make you."

"Are you even sorry?"

Rodrick sighed. "Yes, and no. Without the lies, we wouldn't be as we are now. I wouldn't have gotten to know the truth of you. Just the golden mask you present the world."

"You've ruined me."

"There's a simple solution—"

"Why? How could you sleep with me?"

"Because there is something between us that demands attention! Maid or royal—I'd have you either way. You're just *Valla* to me, not the bleeding sunstar. The girl who survived Jotunfjall against all odds and still had the courage to want more. *You* are enough."

She shook her head vehemently. "You would pin me to the wall like one of your pelts. Just another conquest of the hunt."

He grabbed her shoulders and pulled her closer. "We would hunt together."

"You've ruined any chance we ever had of being together."

"Don't say that. I won't force you, but I would still have you as my wife, Valla."

She pulled away from him and slipped venom into her voice. "We fucked, Rodrick. We didn't read vows. Not a first for either of us." The lid on her anger shook, threatening to boil over. "If you think I would ever marry you, then you're as big a fool as your great uncle."

Rodrick's face tightened, jaw ticking. "You are already my wife in all but name."

Fury chased on the heels of disbelief. Her voice grew thunderous. "Would your *wife* sleep on beds of straw and work her fingers to the bone for your entire court? You let your charade continue until it bloody well near killed me, then swept in to play savior and lured me to your bed."

"*My* charade? You showed up to my home and lied to my face, and I played along rather than exposing you in front of my entire court and forcing you into marriage. Is that what you would have preferred? I've put hundreds of lives at risk for the sake of *your* charade."

Valla scoffed. "Didn't stop you from fucking me."

"That was never part of the plan," he growled.

A new idea emerged, one whispered by her worst insecurities.

Her hand went to her stomach. "Oh sunmother. You've laid your trap well, haven't you? No wonder you were so eager to spend inside me. Start the breeding early, huh? Is that contraceptive tea even effective, or just another part of the plan? How many months pregnant would you ensure I was before revealing you knew?"

She threw the balled-up portrait at him, and it rolled to a stop against his boot. "You'd have all winter to fuck a baby into me, to force me into this marriage one way or another."

Rodrick seethed. "I would never force that on you, Valla. Frieda has no idea who you are. Only Astrid and I know."

Astrid. Of course. Another stab of the knife. The closest thing to a friendly face she'd found here, all because of her status.

"I don't understand, Rodrick. How did you see this playing out? How does this ever end well?"

He scrubbed a hand through his hair, then walked to the window and collapsed in his chair.

"I was angry with you, at first. I thought you a spoiled brat trying to escape the engagement and bring more death to my door. I'll admit, it was entertaining to see my enemy's daughter blacking my hearth, doing my wash. I wanted to watch that infamous Sunstar sheen dull. I wanted you to give up and confess.

"You wanted to break me."

He didn't deny it. "Yes."

"Well, congratulations."

Rodrick scoffed. "You're not so easily broken, Valla. You took the ruse farther than I ever expected you to. I regret how far I let it go, but your strength, gods, even your damnable stubbornness, are some of the things I most admire about you. And my people will recognize and respect that strength when they learn the truth."

She barked out a harsh laugh. "Your people will never respect me. Not after this. I demeaned myself in front of all of them. Let them run roughshod over me. I can never be your queen."

"This isn't Isaana. Respect is earned here, not given. I believe they'd think you quite the clever trickster."

"I nearly died. They want to kill me, Rodrick!"

"Frieda has been dealt with. As will anyone else—harshly. If we do not marry, our people will return to war. Am I to seek a different arrangement? To let the world believe you are dead?"

"So I'm to be the bargaining chip once again. Another man content to dictate my future."

Rodrick let out a heavy sigh. "You are not the only one who was sold for peace. Did you ever stop to consider my feelings about this arrangement? Wonder if I wanted to get married to a stranger, the daughter of my oldest enemy? No?"

The truth was, she hadn't. She'd been much too wrapped up in her own worries.

Rodrick bowed his head into his hands.

"What do you want, Valla?"

"Not this—never any of this. I won't be their martyr. I have been a man's pawn my entire life. This was my chance to finally escape it all. Would you hold me back from that?"

"You know I cannot leave. You can't ask me to abandon my people."

"I know. But I can't do *this*."

"And what was this to you, princess? A dalliance? A bit of northern cock before you start your grand adventure? Something to hold you over till spring, when you run and let the weight of your responsibilities fall to the rest of us?"

"What would you have it be?"

"I want forever."

Valla laughed, half-choking on the sound. "You can't be serious."

His eyes burned.

"I am. I want you, Valla. But you're determined to run away."

"You don't even know me!"

"I know your heart. The way you prefer your coffee. The face you make when you taste a food you dislike but force yourself to chew it anyways. How much you hate mornings and how cold your feet get at night. Your compassion, your drive. Your stubbornness. The way your hair curls after a hot bath. The smell of your skin on my sheets, the weight of you in my arms. The feel of you coming undone on my cock.

"But I would know more."

Fuck. He sounded like a man in love—or a man trying very hard to be convincing.

"This was all meant to be temporary."

"And if you are pregnant? Our time in the cave—"

"I began my bleeding this morning. You need not worry that I'll abscond with your heir. It seems I've escaped the yoke of that burden, despite your best efforts."

It was a lie. Her monthly courses weren't due yet, but she'd been taking the contraceptive tea daily. She couldn't give him any hopes to cling to if she wanted him to let her go.

His face fell. "No child of ours would ever be a burden, Valla."

The sincerity and longing in his gaze were too much. She needed a decisive cut to sever the clinging threads between them. So she aimed her barb and struck true.

"They would be cursed!"

Lightning sparked in Rodrick's eyes, and his face twisted into something dark.

Valla shivered as the temperature in the room plummeted. A crack shot through the ice in the window.

"You are nothing like what I expected, Seraphina. Yet at the end of it all you still manage to be so stunningly disappointing. Your father's daughter after all. I would never condemn my child to a mother clearly so incapable of loving them."

Incapable of loving *him.* The words went unspoken between them, nonetheless infecting the air.

His expression shuttered as he stood up from the chair. "I

came inside you because I liked the squeeze of your tight cunt, but there are plenty of those to be found elsewhere."

Rodrick strode to the door and swung it open, then paused. He took a deep breath.

"Valla— I didn't—"

"No. We're being honest with each other for once, Rodrick. Let's not sully it with more lies."

He was silent for a long time, lingering.

"Do you still intend to let me leave come spring?" she asked.

The muscles in his back flexed. "If that is what you wish."

"I very much wish it."

"Very well."

The door closed behind him with a quiet snick.

A great, wrenching sob filled Valla's chest, and she struggled to shove it down. The tears she'd been holding back were banging at the gate. She crumpled into a heap on the rug and let them fall.

CHAPTER 20
VALLA

Valla started taking meals in her room, occupying her time with walks in the ice garden or reading the books she'd taken from Rodrick's library before their fight. She avoided the Storm King entirely.

Astrid visited her occasionally, but conversation was tense and awkward between them.

They dropped the pretense of Valla being Rodrick's assistant. He didn't call on her, and she didn't seek him out. She still left his coffee with the guards at his door each morning, because not making his cup was just too depressing. It was likely half cold by the time he got to it.

Rodrick's magic was pushing at the edges and leaking out. The weather on the mountain worsened noticeably, and the winds only quieted when he slept or left the keep. There were often sheets of ice left to slowly melt in the halls wherever he traveled.

This morning, a note with breakfast requested her presence in Rodrick's office. Valla dressed and went to him immediately, leaving her food untouched. Her stomach was a mass of nerves.

What did he want?

"Come in," he called when she knocked.

Rodrick didn't look up from his desk when she entered. His quill moved busily across a piece of parchment.

He looked exhausted. Had he not been sleeping well? The loss of so much magic had to be taking a toll on him.

"Good morning," Valla said.

"What is your plan, when you leave?"

Right to it then.

Valla shrugged. "Move elsewhere in Valenmur, or far enough away from Sunstone that none will know me."

Valla hadn't spent much time thinking about the future, if she was honest with herself. She'd been focused on surviving winter undiscovered. A future free from the obligations of her station had always been a nebulous idea; a dream unlikely to ever be realized. But for once in her life, she didn't have to be Princess Seraphina Sunstar. She was Valla, foundling of the north.

"You don't have any money. How will you live?"

"I can learn a trade."

"What trade?"

"I don't know..."

"So you're going to descend Jotunfjall with no money, no trade, no real plan to speak of and just...figure it out? Seems to me that escape itself is more important to you than any partic-ular future."

Valla bristled. "I might fail, but I should be allowed to try. I never had the luxury of figuring out the future I wanted for myself. As you well know."

"Very well. I'll send you with enough funds to get you started. Sufficient to secure you for a year, two if you're frugal."

"You don't—"

He raised his hand to stop her. "Don't argue with me

about this, Valla. A woman alone in the realm needs all the help she can get. And it will make this easier for me."

Valla swallowed. "Make what easier?"

"Letting you go."

"Spring is many months yet—"

"You can take the tunnels at any time."

Valla went quiet. It made sense. Why hadn't she considered that option?

Rodrick flipped to another piece of parchment and continued writing. "You've wanted to leave since you arrived. There's nothing stopping you now."

Valla picked at the aggravated flesh around her cuticles.

"You want me to go? Now?" She didn't know how to feel. She thought there'd be more time for the anger between them to cool.

Rodrick sighed and set down his quill, folding his hands together on the desk. His expression was closed off.

"Our intimacy is breeding rumors. People grow more suspicious by the day, and your father will send an envoy before the snows melt if he wants to keep war from his doorstep. His emissaries will recognize you.

"The tunnels exit near Sunstone. You'd do well to be far away by spring. The longer you wait, the more dangerous it will become."

"Rodrick—"

He picked up the sheet of parchment and shook the ink dry, then slid it across the desk toward her.

"You will take Nanook. She can guide you through the tunnels safely. This is information for one of my contacts in the south. You can leave Nanook there, and I'll collect her come spring."

"I can't—"

"I am being exceedingly accommodating, Princess Seraphina. If you want me to let you go, we will do it my way."

Rodrick's use of her formal name and title took her aback. He was trying to distance himself from her in any way he could.

Valla hadn't forgiven him yet, but she wasn't ready to say goodbye. Would they ever see each other again? Or would their time together fade like a dream upon waking?

Rodrick's dismissal felt like an excuse to be rid of her and the damnable tension between them. One she ought to welcome, if she hadn't gotten so twisted up in him. But they'd come too far for this to just...end. A week ago he'd been holding her in his arms and planning their next winter activity together as they went to sleep.

Valla sighed. This was for the best. Distance would clear both their heads.

"Very well, *my lord*."

THEY PLANNED her departure for a week later. Rodrick mapped what he could of the tunnels from memory, but Valla was to rely on Nanook if the route was unclear.

Valla had packed her things, but unease lay heavy on her mind. She missed Rodrick. His scent, his touch, the feel of him moving inside her. Their intimate conversations late into the night. His breath on her skin.

Goodbye hung between them like a chain neither was eager to tug. Valla needed to be with him one more time before she left Frostheim. One more time, just to get him out of her system.

Valla pulled on a nightrobe and padded on bare feet to Rodrick's rooms. The guards were stationed outside his bedroom overnight, but she'd spent enough time in his chambers that they let her in without complaint. She'd half-feared he would have barred her access.

The room was dark but for a few glowing embers in the hearth. Nanook lay splayed out in front of it. The hound startled awake when the door snicked shut behind Valla, but she settled her head back on her paws once she recognized Valla's scent.

Valla approached the bed. Rodrick was sleeping naked, as he usually did. One of his arms was stretched out towards her side of the bed.

Valla sank a knee into the mattress, and Rodrick's eyes slid open, the spark of his magic lighting up the darkness.

He lunged for her and rolled them over, pinning her beneath him. Then cold metal was pressed against her throat.

Valla's heart thumped frantically in her chest.

Rodrick blinked down at her, recognition slowly dawning.

"Valla? What's wrong? Did something happen?"

She gave a short shake of her head. "I can't leave without saying goodbye."

He rolled off her and slid his blade into a sheath beneath his pillow.

"That was foolish. You could have been killed."

"I can't say I expected that kind of reaction."

"I'm not used to people skulking about my bed chamber at night. Especially without Nanook alerting me."

"Sorry. I wasn't thinking."

His eyes were guarded as he looked at her. "Why are you here?"

She wanted to reach her hand across the space separating them. She didn't know how to bridge the gap.

"I told you—"

"I don't want to hear it. I *can't* hear it."

Valla swallowed past the thickness in her throat and slid her hand up his muscled thigh. "One more time? For old time's sake?"

Rodrick scoffed. "For old time's sake? We'd barely gotten started."

"I want you. I want to remember this."

"Show me."

"What?"

"Show me how badly you want it. Since you're so determined to give it up."

Valla narrowed her gaze on him and crawled on top of him.

Rodrick gripped her thighs and slid her even closer. "Lose the gown."

Valla unknotted the tie at her waist and shrugged the gown off her shoulders, revealing her naked body underneath. His breath hissed.

"You walked here wearing that?"

She settled atop his lap, her core hot against his quickly stiffening cock. She rolled her hips against him.

"I was in a hurry."

Rodrick's head knocked back against the headboard. "Who's on duty tonight? I need to make note of it so I can be sure to cut their eyes out later."

Valla smiled and leaned forward to kiss him, but Rodrick turned his cheek.

"No kissing. This isn't about that."

His refusal stung, but she couldn't fault him for it. And she wouldn't risk losing these final moments between them to an argument.

She reached between their bodies and took his cock in hand, pumping it a few times.

Rodrick hissed, and his fingers dug into her hips. "I'm not in the mood to be nice tonight, Valla."

"I don't need you to be nice. I need you to fuck me."

His hand fisted in the back of her hair, eyes hardening on her. "Then suck."

Valla slid down his body and lowered her mouth to his cock, giving the head a tentative lick.

She glanced back up at him. "I've never done this before." She was familiar with the mechanics, but not the execution.

His grip on her hair tightened. "Good. Open."

Valla parted her lips, and he thrust into her mouth, pushing her head down to meet his hips.

She gagged a little at the sudden intrusion. Her nails dug into his thighs as she fit her tongue against the base of his shaft. He'd given her most of his length, the head nudging at the back of her throat.

There was something in her that craved the brutality of his actions. She wanted him to leave his mark on her—for tonight to be unforgettable.

"Breathe through your nose. Relax your throat."

Valla calmed herself and did as he instructed, surprised when the tickling sensation from a throat full of cock faded.

"Good girl. Now suck."

She tightened her lips around him and slid up to the head, then up and down his shaft. Several passes later, she was comfortable trying to take him as deep as she could. She buried her nose against his pelvis until her eyes watered.

"Fuck, Valla. That's it."

She alternated her mouth with her tongue, licking up his shaft and around the glans until his hips began to buck and he was thrusting her throat full.

She tasted precum on her tongue, and Rodrick began directing her head how he wanted, fucking himself with her mouth.

His roughness turned her on, and she ground herself against the hard muscle of his thigh, wetting him with her arousal.

Rodrick growled and pulled her up off his cock, his grip

on her hair tight enough to burn. "I want to cum down your throat, but I want that pussy even more."

Valla was a mess. Dripping on his thigh, face smeared with saliva, hair in disarray.

"So fucking pretty," he said, smearing her lower lip with his thumb. He pulled it back, and a string of saliva stretched between them.

Rodrick took his cock in hand, big and pulsing with need, and slid his palm up and down it. "Come here. I want to fuck you."

Valla crawled up his body to straddle his lap. Rodrick released his cock, and it sprung up, smacking against her clit.

She rose up on her knees and slid him inside her. The stretch burned, and she tossed her head back as she struggled to take all of him.

His hand went to her clit as she worked herself on his cock, but his motions were mechanical, his eyes detached. He was already pulling away from her, closing himself off behind a wall of ice.

She grasped his face as he moved inside her, forcing him to meet her eyes. "Stay with me. Please. Be with me in this moment."

Rodrick shut his eyes for several long seconds, and when they opened again, the pain in them was unmistakable.

Then he took her mouth in a kiss that said everything they wouldn't.

It was the most intense sex they'd had yet, their bodies in conversation with each other as they held eye contact.

Valla looked away first. It was too much. Too intimate.

Rodrick fed his fingers into her mouth, and she sucked at them until they were dripping.

Then he spread the lubrication between the cleft of her ass, circling the ring of muscle there.

Valla stiffened. The sensation was odd, but not unpleasant.

"I want to touch you here," he huffed into her ear.

"Do it," Valla said, her body tensing up.

Rodrick ran his other hand up and down her spine, stroking it in a soothing motion. "Relax. I won't hurt you. Keep riding me."

Valla started moving again, and the feeling of his cock stretching her open as she slid up and down distracted her from her concerns.

Rodrick slowly worked his smallest finger into her ass as she rode him. It was uncomfortable at first, but that faded as he introduced more lubricant into her tight channel.

"Fuck," she moaned.

The foreign sensation amplified everything else. She'd never felt so full.

"More."

His cock swelled inside her. He swapped to his middle finger after wetting it with more spit, then slid it in past the second knuckle.

She braced her hands on his shoulders, hair hanging in his face as she moved, and Rodrick slipped his finger in and out of her ass.

"Gods. I can feel myself inside you. You're tightening around me so nicely, Valla. Do you want to come?"

She jerked her head in a nod. She felt so full, so close to bursting at the edges and coming apart atop his cock and fingers.

Rodrick slid a second finger into her ass as he stroked her clit and thrust up into her.

Valla shattered as he fucked both her holes into submission. She clung to him, nails diggings into his chest as her hips jerked and her pussy spasmed around him.

Rodrick popped his fingers out of her ass, then gripped

her hips and rolled her over beneath him. He slid Valla's hands above her head and held them there.

There was no break in his thrusts. He was hitting even deeper now, his strokes rough, almost cruel.

"Who made you come, Valla?"

"You did," she moaned. She was tossing her head back and forth, still riding out the sensation of that explosive orgasm.

"Louder. Let everyone know who you belong to."

He changed the angle of his hips and thrust even deeper.

"Rodrick!" she screamed.

His magic, leashed till now, began to pulse throughout the room. He must be close.

"Finish inside me," Valla said. This couldn't be the end. She needed—wanted to keep him with her.

"What?" His breath was ragged.

"It's safe. I've been taking the tea."

His eyes hardened on her. "No. You don't get to ask for that anymore."

"My mouth, then."

"Hells. Hurry."

Rodrick pulled out of her, and Valla slid down the bed between his thighs. As soon as she opened, he was between her lips and thrusting down her throat.

"Yes. Take it."

She could taste herself on him. He fisted his hands in her hair, hips bucking forward as he began to spurt on her tongue. It was thick and salty and there was so, so much of it.

His cock finished emptying inside her, and she swallowed down his come and licked him clean, pumping him to get the last few drops.

They were both breathing heavily, sweaty and gross with sex. Valla just wanted to curl up in his sheets and pass out, but she didn't think Rodrick would allow that.

But when she slid her legs over the side of the bed to leave,

Rodrick pulled her back against his chest and wrapped his arms around her.

"Stay."

In his arms. On his mountain. She knew he meant both.

"Rodrick—"

"What more do you want? Is this not enough? I'll give you everything."

"You know I can't."

He let out a heavy sigh. "I want to beg you to stay. But I know you will not."

There was a substantial part of her that did want to stay with him, but abandoning her plan now felt like sacrificing some part of herself she'd never get back.

"I will miss you. More than I could have possibly imagined."

"Speak not of goodbyes, please."

Valla swallowed her tears. Leaving him was going to feel like ripping her heart out of her chest and surrendering it to winter's bite.

Rodrick pulled her onto his chest and stroked from the crown of her hair down her back, over and over again.

"Go to sleep, little sunstar. Do not cry."

AT SOME POINT in the middle of the night, Valla stirred when Rodrick's weight lifted off the bed. She rolled over to see him kneeling by the hearth, stroking Nanook's head.

"Take care of her, girl. Be brave and strong. I'll see you again soon."

Valla's heart cracked. She closed her eyes and forced herself back into sleep.

When she woke the second time, early morning sun broke through the window. She rolled over to discover Rodrick's side of the bed empty and long cold.

A note rested on his pillow. Valla reached for it and scrubbed the sleep out of her eyes.

I can't watch you leave. Good luck, Valla. You will be great at whatever you choose.

Tears bubbled in her throat, but she choked them back. She couldn't cry today. Not until she was out of the keep, with only Nanook for company.

Her heart was heavy as she woke, dressed, and gathered her things. An hour later, Astrid fetched her from her rooms.

Things were moving too quickly. She wasn't ready to say goodbye. She was finally getting what she'd wanted for so long, so why was she beginning to question whether she wanted it at all? When confronted with the reality of it, her freedom felt hollow.

"Everything is ready," Astrid said. The shieldmaiden was tight-lipped this morning, and Valla could tell she wanted to say more than she did.

Astrid escorted her to the courtyard, where a saddled elk and Nanook awaited. Valla's pack had straps that let it be worn on her back for ease while traveling, and Nanook was buckled into her supply harness.

Nanook laid down and sat her head on her paws. Her expression was dejected, as if she knew she was leaving her master. Rodrick seldom went anywhere without her.

Valla smoothed her hand through the fur behind the hound's ears. "I'm sorry, darling. It'll be okay. I'll take good care of you, and you'll see your father again soon."

Valla investigated the contents of Nanook's satchels, adding them to her mental tally of supplies.

Rodrick had gone overboard. There was water and rations for a trip three times as long, as well as packets of dried kindling for starting fires, fur blankets, and a tent. Plus the gold. His estimate had been conservative. She could live off it for three years, in the cheaper parts of Valenmur. Enough to buy her own place and take her time figuring out what she wanted to do with her life.

She would never have been able to carry it all without Nanook's strong back.

Valla tied the satchel closed and busied herself adjusting Nanook's harness. She was running out of tasks to stall her departure, and Rodrick was still nowhere to be seen.

"Where is he?" Valla asked Astrid.

"Somewhere torturing himself. You two—ugh." Astrid shook her head. "Just go, if that's truly your desire. If you wait any longer, he's liable to change his mind about letting you leave." She cast a concerned glance at the sky. "Weather's already turning to shit."

Valla mounted the elk with Astrid's help. "Thank you. For your friendship."

Astrid patted the elk on the rump. "Safe travels, princess. Write me, once you get to where you're going. It will put his mind at ease."

Valla nodded, and she was off.

CHAPTER 21
RODRICK

She was gone.

She was gone, and she wasn't coming back.

In the end, there'd been no last minute love confessions, no begging or tears. Just the silence of a cold winter morning they'd both weathered alone.

Rodrick had never laid his heart bare to anyone before, and it'd been for nothing, in the end.

Had he tried hard enough? Said enough of the right things and few enough wrong ones? He'd never had a connection with a woman that ran so deep before, excepting his mother— and that had ended tragically, too.

Valla left no part of her behind to cling to—had brought nothing with her to begin with. In and out of his life like a ghost.

Had she even been real, or just a grand delusion?

That's where Astrid found him. Marinating in melancholy and dragon's milk in his office, staring into his hearthfire like it'd personally aggrieved him.

Astrid sighed and sunk into his spare chair. "You're really

letting her leave? With your dog, no less? No romantic chase through the tunnels planned?"

"I don't want to talk about this, Astrid."

Astrid rapped a knuckle on the ice block filling the window. "This is the worst storm I've seen since your mother died. I had the grooms stable the animals and called in the gate guard. You're liable to drown us all in snow by week's end."

He grunted. "Not your worst idea."

"Even the elders are whispering about jotun önd."

"Giant's breath? They're superstitious old fools. I have it under control."

Astrid rolled her eyes. "Why are you letting her leave? Go after her. She will travel slow. You know those tunnels like the back of your hand."

"I can't."

"Then let me. I'll drag her back by the hair, kicking and screaming, and force her to marry you!"

Rodrick's lips turned up. "A wonderful foundation for a marriage, I'm sure."

"Well your plan seems to be going swimmingly."

"Wasn't it you who said I'd catch more snowcats with treats?"

Astrid snorted. "Clearly I underestimated her stubbornness. Time to get out the stick."

"Didn't your father ever tell you that if you truly love something, you'll let it go?"

"No, he didn't, because it's advice for soft-hearted fools. He was a fisherman with six hungry mouths to feed. He believed that if you loved something, you'd stick it with a spear and have it for supper."

Astrid sighed and kicked her feet up onto the ottoman.

"Why'd you let her leave? Aside from the war, the betrothal—you obviously care for her."

"It has to be her choice. I couldn't force her to stay and to marry me. She would chafe against such restraints, and one day rid herself of them entirely. I don't want her wondering 'what if' the rest of her life."

"You're both fools. She asked me about a contraceptive. How could you risk that?"

"Because I'm a bloody fool, okay?"

"And you're absolutely sure she's not—"

"She's not. She bled."

Astrid huffed out a breath. "Okay. Do you know where she's heading, at least?"

"She's leaving Nanook with one of our contacts in the south. He'll know to put a tail on her."

Astrid shook her head. "Gods, men are stupid."

Valla

THE TRIP up the mountain to the beacon was lonely. Even Nanook wasn't her usual rambunctious self. A storm was brewing in the distance, heading straight for the keep, but the wind was already here. It whipped at her clothes and bit at her skin. They fought against it with each step forward. Like even the weather was telling her to turn around.

When they reached the peak, Valla dismounted her elk and sent it back down the pass with a click of her tongue and a pat on the bum. It wouldn't do for him to be caught out in the storm.

The entrance to the tunnels was already open, and a disc of ice coated in a fine layer of snow filled the shaft.

The feelings Valla had been suppressing over the last few days welled up in her chest, threatening to overflow. Rodrick had been here this morning. She hadn't even accounted for how she would get Nanook down the ladder, but he'd thought of everything.

She urged Nanook onto the disc and fisted her hand in the fur of her neck. The disc began to rotate and descend, lowering them into darkness.

Rodrick had estimated it would take them a week to travel south via the tunnels. Still far quicker than the three week trek up Jotunfjall during winter's onset, but she wasn't keen on being stuck beneath the earth for so long. Especially when her sole companions were a tundra hound, the eerie creaking of the ice, and whatever creatures dwelled in the darkness.

The tunnels were more ominous without Rodrick's reassuring presence. Each pebble of ice sent skittering or unexplained noise echoing ahead of them made her heart race.

Nanook stayed close by her side, and Valla talked to her to fill the silence and distract herself from getting lost in maudlin thoughts. She had to keep reminding herself that this was what she'd wanted.

They made good progress, only stopping to sleep for a few hours when Valla grew too exhausted to continue.

When they slept, Valla curled up beneath one of Rodrick's furs and used Nanook's soft belly as a pillow. She didn't once dream, as if they were too deep within the earth for her to reach the realm of sleep.

A few days into their journey, Valla slipped on a patch of ice and folded her ankle. Putting weight on it ached. She contemplated turning back north then, but the tunnels had tended to slope downward the further south they got. Going back would be twice as arduous.

Eventually ice began to recede to stone, and the air warmed.

The path ended when the tunnel narrowed into an ominous, steeply sloping chute. There'd be no returning if she went down it.

Valla couldn't even see the bottom. For all she knew, it might open up into a bottomless pit or a frozen lake. Spikes of ice or stone could be lining the dark tunnel, ready to skewer her.

Nanook gave her a plaintive look.

"Nothing ventured, nothing gained—right girl?"

Nanook went first, her belly crouched low against the rock. Valla only had the skittering of her claws to mark her descent.

She waited a minute before following. She climbed into the tunnel legs first, holding her arms tight against her sides to keep her frame narrow. Then Valla pushed off.

Her hair and clothes snagged against the rough gravel as she skidded forward. Then the slope steepened further, the stone smoothing out, and she was sliding faster and faster.

A light appeared in the distance. Valla lifted her chest to see.

Then her head smacked into something hard, and a splinter of pain shot through her skull.

The floor of the tunnel disappeared out from beneath her, and she was falling. She landed on her ass, and a shudder of pain snaked up her tailbone.

Voices echoed around her. Her head throbbed.

"Who's there?" someone called.

She winced, her vision blurry. Something wet dripped into her eye. Light pierced the gloom.

Then a glowing ball of fire was held up to her face, Stefan's twisted grin lit behind it.

"Hello, princess."

CHAPTER 22
VALLA

Valla woke to warmth. It was too much. Sweat pooled on her back and beaded her brow. Rodrick must have piled furs on her in addition to his considerable body heat.

She twisted around, trying to escape the heat. A splitting headache pounded behind her eyes.

Thin fingers gripped at her, the nails sharp and unfamiliar. A shadow loomed overhead.

Valla tried to pull away, but she was trapped. She forced her eyes open.

Stefan bent over her, her wrist trapped in his hand as he traced invisible designs on her forearm. Her skin burned where he touched.

This had to be a nightmare. Stefan was dead.

Valla scrambled up the bed until her back was flush against the headboard. Stefan tightened his grip on her wrist.

A female voice said, "Valla, it's okay. You're safe now."

Valla jerked her head to the left. Evangeline, her middle sister, hovered by her bed. Her face crinkled with worry.

"Where am I?"

"You're home. You're safe."

Valla clenched her eyes shut, willing this nightmare to end. When she opened them back up, the painted ceiling of her bedroom in the Sun Palace stared down at her.

"No." The events of yesterday began to rush back in. She cast her eyes around the room. "Where's Nanook? Where is she?"

"What'd you do with the dog, Stefan?" Evangeline asked.

"The mutt's in a cage in the kennels. She's lucky I didn't barbeque her after she tried to take a piece out of me."

"Let me go!" Valla yanked at Stefan's grip, and this time he released her.

"What were you doing with the Storm King's beast? I recognize it from the battlefield."

"Enough, Stefan!" Evangeline barked. "Have someone bring the dog from the kennels. She's distressed enough as it is."

Valla's thoughts were cloudy and panicked. She tried to recall the series of events that'd led here, searched for the last thing she remembered. Sliding down the tunnel, a searing pain in her head—then voices and Stefan's grinning face.

She rose a hand to her forehead and found her hairline crusty with blood and sore to the touch. Eva tutted and lowered Valla's hand.

"Don't touch. It's only just stopped bleeding. The doctor will be here soon."

Cold fear slithered down Valla's spine. They knew where the entrance to the tunnels was. She had to write Rodrick, had to warn him—

Evangeline pressed the back of her cool hand to Valla's forehead. "You're burning up. Stefan, what are you doing? Send for the doctor and fetch the animal. Now!"

Stefan's nose wrinkled, but he obeyed.

As soon as the door shut, Evangeline pulled her into a tight hug, burying Valla's face in her generous breasts.

"Oh, Valla. I've missed you so. What happened? We heard you were dead—lost in the snows. Cora and I cried for weeks."

"How did I get here?"

"A group of soldiers found you wandering around the foot of the mountain with a head wound, and they sent for Stefan. He brought you in two days ago, but you've been insensate."

"They're lying. Stefan was there. He found me."

"You hit your head, Valla. You might be confused—"

"Does father know I'm here?"

Eva gave a tight nod.

Valla swallowed. This couldn't be happening. She was right back where she'd started. The last place she wanted to be. Her father would be livid. Worse than a dead daughter was one that eschewed her duty, in his mind.

Valla glanced around the room again. She was surprised her youngest sister wasn't here with Eva.

"Where's Cora?"

Eva's eyes fell. "In her rooms. She was branded a few days ago."

Valla sucked in her breath through her nose. "That bastard. Was it Stefan?"

Eva nodded.

"I thought that firefucker had died in the avalanche."

"What happened in Frostheim, Valla? Everyone is very confused."

Valla chewed her lip. She didn't know how to explain it, the most advantageous route to take, now that she was back in this pit of snakes. "I promise I'll tell you the whole story eventually, Eva. But I need to think."

Eva nodded, accepting her prevarication for now. "Father will demand answers soon. He has his radiant guards posted outside your room. I'll do what I can to help you, but things in the palace are tense right now. No one is sure what your return means for the alliance with Frostheim."

The bedroom door swung open, ushering in Renfrew, the head palace doctor. He wore red robes, an ornate headpiece, and a flaming sun wrought in gold on a chain around his neck.

"Princess. I'm glad to see you're awake."

"I'm fine. I was just exhausted from my travels."

"Your...travels. Right. I must examine you. You took quite the bump on your head. You might have a concussion."

Valla nodded.

Renfrew palpated her forehead with his papery hands and tsked. "Quite a lot of bruising, but the cut's shallow. Lucky. Head wounds can be quite the bleeders."

He pried her upper and lower eyelids open with his fingers and stared at her pupils. Then he tottered around the bed, pulling out a number of instruments from his many-pocketed robe to prod her with.

"Your temperature is concerning."

Valla nodded. "It's too hot in here. Please douse the fires." Some mad man had lit several braziers around the room.

Eva and Renfrew glanced at each other, twin frowns on their faces.

"You feel warm?" Renfrew asked.

"Boiling."

"Your skin's cold as ice, Valla," Eva said.

Renfrew hummed. "Your body adjusting to the drastic change in temperatures, perhaps. We'll monitor it closely in the coming days. Have you had your menses recently?"

Valla stiffened. She knew what he was really asking—did she return to Sunstone with Frostheim's heir in her belly?

"Yes," she lied.

"Very well. I'm assigning you bedrest and lots of fluids. And I know you feel warm, but your body temperature is dangerously low. The fires will stay, for now."

Valla suppressed a groan. Her blanket was already half-drenched with sweat. She wanted to strip off her clothes and the bedding and lay as still as possible until she began to cool down.

The door opened again, admitting a familiar ball of white fluff. Upon spotting Valla, Nanook charged forward, yanking the reed-shaped boy holding her chain through the doorway. The boy tripped forward and released the leash as Nanook leapt onto the bed with a delighted yip.

Nanook gave Valla's cheek an exuberant lick before circling her legs and laying down. The hound's body spanned the foot of the bed.

Sunmother, she'd gone and managed to steal Rodrick's dog as well. She'd have to find a way to get her out of the palace and to Rodrick's contact. No small feat, with the eyes of the entire court on her.

"Princess—the animal is unsanitary—" Renfrew reached for her dangling chain, and Nanook lunged forward and bared her teeth in a fierce growl. The doctor scampered back, and Valla gave Nanook an encouraging pat.

"*She stays*," Valla said, turning on her princess voice for the first time in an age.

Eva nodded. "She's protective of you."

"Fine, but if she disturbs your rest—"

"You're the one disturbing my rest, currently."

Renfrew straightened and brushed imaginary dust off his robes. "Very well. Princess Eva, I know you're excited by your sister's return from the dead, but she needs to rest. Come."

'*Later,*' Eva mouthed at Valla before following Renfrew through the door.

Valla buried her head in her pillow and screamed.

CHAPTER 23

VALLA

The room was stifling, and sharing a bed with an overzealous dog still sporting her winter coat wasn't helping. Valla used her pitcher of drinking water to douse the flaming braziers. It made the temperature only slightly more tolerable.

Nanook didn't seem overly troubled by the heat, which was odd. Valla was soaking through her shift with sweat, and the hound wasn't even panting.

Valla tried the door and windows, hoping to air out the room, and found them both locked from the outside.

"Fuck!" She stamped her foot on the ground. She was truly her father's prisoner once more.

She needed to get out of here. Her father would already be plotting, preparing to march her back to Frostheim or use her as a pawn in his bargaining with Rodrick. She didn't want to be used against him—and she *needed* to warn him that her father knew of the southern entrance to the tunnels.

How had they figured it out? Was there a traitor in Rodrick's court? Or perhaps a prisoner from the war had divulged the information? Once they blasted through that steep rock slide and mapped their way through the tunnels, they could attack Frostheim completely by surprise.

One day bled into the next, and Valla remained trapped in her rooms. She missed Rodrick, the heat was intolerable, and she was bored out of her skull. Even her books—her staunchest companions when she'd been banished to her rooms by her father in the past—had been removed.

She relished the times Eva and Cora came by to visit, but they were always too brief. They were inevitably ushered out by the guards, citing the doctor's orders that Valla rest.

Her father was trying to sweat her out, make her soft and pliable for his schemes. She was familiar with his tactics. One of his favorite methods of torture was leaving a prisoner to bake in the sun for days, until their skin began to blister and weep.

When she asked her guards for paper and pen, she was told she shouldn't stress her mind with composition.

More like they didn't want her sneaking any messages out. Eva was able to secret her a few books, parchment, and a quill that Valla kept hidden beneath her mattress during the day. When she was too restless to sleep, she read by moonlight.

Her own body felt alien to her. Like she didn't belong here, and the oppressive heat was sapping her energy. She never thought she'd long for one of Rodrick's ice baths, but she was beginning to recall them fondly. Had it always been this hot here? Had she forgotten so quickly?

She felt stifled, body and soul. Renfrew wouldn't even allow her coffee, and she spent her first two weeks of captivity nursing a splitting headache from the withdrawals.

Valla dreamt of Rodrick every night. In her dreams, he worshiped her body and bathed her in snow, gracing her with a few blessed moments of cold. She longed to wake and find herself in his arms, to discover this had all been a prolonged nightmare. Was this her punishment for leaving, for seeking a different life?

After one such dream, Valla awoke to a chill in the air. She shivered and pulled the blanket up to her chin, wrapping it tighter around her.

Something cold and wet hit her face, and Valla blinked. Then she jerked up, mouth going slack.

Snow was falling from the painted ceiling of her bedroom. Had been for some time, based on the fine layer of powder atop her bedsheets.

Relief swelled within her. It was a sign. Was Rodrick nearby? Had he come for her?

Valla scooped up a handful of snow and buried her face in it. Blessedly cold. She felt well—truly well—for the first time since she'd woken up in the palace. Nanook rolled on her back at the end of the bed, tongue lolling. Contentment swept through her, flooding her veins—

The door opened to admit a maid carrying Valla's breakfast tray. The girl's eyes went wide, and her hands flew to her mouth. The glass tray hit the tile floor and shattered. Fruit rolled in several directions.

"Wait!" Valla called.

But the maid was gone, slamming the door shut behind her. Valla hopped out of bed and shook the snow off the blanket, dispersing it. She drug one of the heavy iron braziers the doctor had insisted on relighting toward the bed, urging it to melt the snow even as the heat sent a roil of nausea twisting through her.

She kicked another pile under the bed as footsteps pounded outside. More flakes continued to drift down from the ceiling.

What was causing it? Could Rodrick really be nearby? Was *she* causing it? He'd left that tiny kernel of his magic inside her, but nothing like this had ever happened before.

Valla stepped as far as she could from the brazier and took several calming breaths. She tried to recall that feeling of peace when she'd first awoke, with her skin chilled and a blanket of snow settled atop her. The flurries slowed to a stop.

Her door swung open to admit Renfrew. His face was red, and he was still in his night clothes.

"Princess," he panted. "I've heard a most disturbing report."

"Oh?"

"Yes. Of snow falling from the ceiling."

Valla snorted. "In this climate? I shook out my pillows, and it sent fluff floating everywhere. I mean really, shouldn't that be the maid's job?"

Renfrew's tiny eyes narrowed on hers.

"Have you had any contact with your husband?"

"My—" They didn't know that she wasn't married? Perhaps her father was trying to save face.

She shook her head. "No."

"Curious."

"Yes, it is curious that I've been assigned a maid who would make such wild claims. The heat must be getting to her."

"I told her to look for signs."

Valla swallowed thickly. "Signs of what?"

"Signs that you're pregnant with the Storm King's child."

Valla froze. *What?*

Several things happened at once.

Valla began counting back the days to her last period, sickening dread twisting her gut. The contraceptive—she'd taken the contraceptive—

That Frieda had given her.

Oh sunmother.

Valla's hand went to her flat belly.

Then the door opened, and Stefan walked in the room.

A strong gust whipped through the curtains, making them billow.

The snow started to fall again, fast and furious, quickly piling up on the mosaic tiles.

"What in the desert hells—"

Renfrew snapped his fingers at Stefan. "Leave, fire mage. You're distressing her."

Stefan cast a long glance around the room, eyes narrowing on Valla, then stepped out.

Valla's breaths heaved. She couldn't get enough air. Nanook whined beside her.

This couldn't be happening. She couldn't be—

"You need to calm down, princess. Stress isn't good for the babe."

"The—babe—" She glanced down at the hand cradled protectively over her lower abdomen.

"No," she whispered.

"Unless the Storm King is outside your window, I'm afraid yes, Princess Seraphina. Your father will be overjoyed at the news."

"No! It's not possible." Had Frieda tampered with her contraceptive tea, or had she just been unlucky? She and Rodrick hadn't exactly been careful when they first started sleeping together.

Renfrew tilted his head. "Are we going with miraculous conception, then?"

"No—I—*fuck.*"

"That is one way it can happen, yes."

The snow fell faster, and Nanook growled low in her throat.

This was not part of the plan. This was one thousand leagues from being part of the plan.

"I'll need to do a proper examination, and your diet will need to be adjusted. Now that the pregnancy is confirmed, we'll get you a daily allotment of fresh air. No sense being cooped up all day."

Now that the pregnancy is confirmed?

"You can't tell him. You can't tell my father. He'll—he'll kill the child. He'll kill me."

"Nonsense. His daughter is carrying the heir of Frostheim. One with the power of the frost heart. He'll take this as wonderful news."

Her breaths came faster now. Her father would turn her child into a pawn. Would brand them as his own. With their heir in his grasp, he could kill Rodrick and have a claim to Frostheim's throne.

Wind whipped through her hair as it whistled through the room. The snow turned into sharp shards of ice.

Renfrew took Valla by the shoulders and led her towards the bed. "Seraphina. You need to calm down. You need to be strong for the child, and creating a blizzard in your room isn't good for anyone's health. I'll send for your sisters."

She gripped Renfrew's arms and stared into his eyes. "Don't tell him, please. I—let me do it."

Renfrew sighed. "You know as well as I that I'd risk my life and that of my family to withhold this information. Besides, there will be no hiding the signs." He gestured vaguely at the room. "This is just the beginning."

CHAPTER 24

VALLA

The next morning, a thick layer of fog blanketed the floor of Valla's bedroom, and more snow coated her bed. The sky was still in morning's gloam outside her window, but the turning of her stomach had awoken her early.

Her stomach flipped again, and Valla scrambled for her chamber pot and emptied her guts into it. She cradled the brass pot and took several deep breaths until her insides began to settle.

One of the guards opened the door while she was still holding the pot. Valla didn't have the energy to shoot him an irate glance.

"His brightness requests an audience with you, princess."

Fuck.

She'd known her father would call for her eventually. It was only a matter of time, now that she had something he wanted.

The Sun King awaited her in his courtroom, where he sat atop his gilded throne, ready to dispense judgment. He'd never interacted with her any other way, even as a child. Always at a distance, always with a cold remove. Without her sisters and the occasional kind maid or governess, her childhood would have been entirely devoid of warmth.

Her father wore his court robes and crown. They glittered in the shaft of sunlight that lit the throne through the glass dome overhead.

He looked the same as he always did. Rich copper skin and short black hair he dyed regularly to hide his greys. His robes were made of a diaphanous golden fabric that seemed to float when he moved.

"Daughter. I am pleased to see you alive. Though I'll admit to some confusion, given the news of your death."

Valla folded her arms behind her back to hide their shaking and gave her father a deferential nod. This was one eventuality she and Rodrick hadn't prepared for. She didn't know what cards to play now that the entire deck had been shuffled.

"A misunderstanding, I fear. My arrival at the Storm King's keep was delayed by an avalanche, as Stefan can attest."

"What was your relationship with the Fjallgard boy? You do not wear his ring."

"We did not wed."

"This is a decision you came to…jointly?"

"Yes. I left with his blessing."

Her father arched his brow. "Yet you carry his child."

There was little sense denying it. Renfrew was right—the signs were only just beginning.

Valla nodded.

"We have friends in the north, you know. Allies who would see this war ended, one way or another. They sent reports of an Isaanan servant the Fjallgard grew close with. But no servants traveled north with you, daughter."

Valla swallowed thickly. Where was he getting his information from? News in and out of the north was difficult during winter. Messenger birds struggled in the cold winds. There were prisoners taken during the war that might have revealed the location of the tunnels, but this was new information.

Her father tapped the arms of his throne.

"You must return to that northern brute and marry him properly this time. There can be no doubt as to the child's legitimacy. Better yet, I will summon him here. Wouldn't want you getting lost in the snows again."

Valla shook her head. "He will not marry me."

"We'll see about that. A man can overcome much when his spawn is involved."

Valla's stomach turned. If Rodrick came to the palace, he'd be walking into a viper's nest.

"Did you know, dear daughter, that the northern power passes down the male line? You have a king in your belly. I may have been cursed to spawn only daughters, but you...your son could rule both realms. And I through him."

Valla grit her teeth. "I will never let that happen."

"And who, pray tell, is going to stop me? You will not be stepping a toe outside the palace until you give birth."

Valla sunk to her knees in front of him. The hard tile ground into her kneecaps. She was loath to beg, but she had to try.

"Please, father. If you've a speck of love for me in that burnt heart of yours, you will not do this."

The Sun King scoffed. "You speak of love? I am granting you a *kingdom*." He flung his hand at her. "You've always been an ungrateful brat. You are dismissed."

When Valla returned to her rooms, she frantically began writing to Rodrick. She wasted several pages when her tears smudged the ink past legibility. Snow fell heavy in her room, and Nanook nosed at her knees as she wrote, sensing her anxiety.

. . .

RODRICK,

I hope this letter finds you well.

My father has written to you claiming that I am pregnant. You'll be relieved to hear that is a lie. He will bid you to come marry me, but I've no more interest in marriage now than when I left.

It's a ruse meant to lure you south unprepared. You know well my father's tricks, and are personally acquainted with my family's talent for lies.

Please do not come. It is a trap. Or if you must treat with him at winter's end, ensure you come prepared for a fight.

I must warn you. There is a traitor among your court. My father knows of the tunnels, and more. His information is current.

I swear I did not tell him. They found me at the tunnel's mouth when I arrived in Isaana.

I know it is not the grand adventure I hoped for, but I am content enough here for now. I've enjoyed my return to the riches I am accustomed to.

Nanook says hello. She is well, though her shedding is outrageous. I haven't yet had time to deliver her to your contact. I will keep her safe until she can rejoin you—hopefully before the heat of summer arrives.

She misses you.

Regards,

Valla

WHEN EVA NEXT VISITED HER, Valla slipped the letter into her sister's pocket.

"Please get this to him, Eva. Whatever you have to do. I've included the information for one of his contacts in Isaana. I have to warn him—to tell him it's a trap. He can't come here. Father will kill him."

Eva frowned down at Valla. "And what of the babe?"

"The babe will be better served by not being fashioned into father's political puppet. If we don't wed, the child will have no claim to Frostheim's throne."

"Do you love him, Valla?"

"The baby? I—"

"The Storm King."

Valla screwed her eyes shut, but tears leaked out. "I think I might."

Eva looked at her with a pitying expression. "Very well. I will do all I can, sister."

CHAPTER 25
VALLA

Pregnancy was miserable. After two weeks of morning sickness, Valla was down ten pounds and had no energy. She wished she had someone to ask about what was happening to her body. A woman—not Renfrew, who was solely her father's creature. She couldn't keep food down, her breasts were tender, and she often woke with a splitting headache. Her body temperature vacillated between too cold and too hot—never just right, making her scowl at the little winter mage in her belly. This was surely their doing.

Valla's hand slid over her stomach. There were procedures —magical and mundane—that could rid a woman of their child in the early months. But she'd always wanted to be a mother, she'd just never imagined having to reckon with the reality of a child so soon. It'd always been a far off concept, one she hadn't spent any time mentally preparing for.

Part of her thrilled that she carried a piece of Rodrick inside her, while another found it arcane that she was now sharing her body with someone else.

She wouldn't keep it secret from Rodrick forever. Once the danger had passed, she'd write to him and tell him. She wanted to give the child the stable family unit she'd been deprived of, and she'd try her damnedest accomplish that, even if it meant living on Rodrick's bloody mountain.

He would make a fantastic father. He'd have the kid bundled up in furs, making snow patterns and packing snowballs before they could walk. He'd perch them between his thighs on the saddle and teach them to ride horses and elk alike.

But it was foolish to be picturing her child's future in the north. Her plan was shaky at best. There was no guarantee she'd escape her father. No guarantee Rodrick would want her or the babe at all. And by circumventing their marriage, Valla was divesting herself of the very bonds that would guarantee her and the child a secure future.

The next six months would require a careful political waltz if she didn't want her family to end up beneath her father's golden boots. Escaping had to be a priority. Because even if her father failed to make the marriage happen, he would use the child as a pawn—either as leverage to control her and Rodrick, or for the power they possessed.

Valla stilled as realization bloomed. The baby had clearly inherited the frost heart. Would prolonged time in the south affect their health? Was the curse in effect prior to their birth? Was that why her side effects were so egregious, or was this the norm for a magical pregnancy?

She had so many questions. There were too many unknowns, but Valla couldn't even communicate her fears to the doctor without exposing Rodrick's weakness.

As the weeks passed, worry gnawed at Valla. Her appetite worsened with every bout of morning sickness. She tried to eat, for the baby's sake, but nothing would stay down.

The melancholy was contagious. Even Nanook, usually bursting with energy, slept most of the day and needed to be cajoled into finishing her meals.

Valla was allowed a daily walk amongst the palace gardens —much like a dog on a leash. She was heavily escorted by guards who refused to talk to her. She enjoyed Nanook's company, but the hound could only do so much to combat the maw of loneliness eating away at Valla.

The gardens were one of the few places the harem ladies were allowed to roam—though not during Valla's walks, of course. Their separation from the rest of the palace was vigilantly maintained.

As a child, when Valla wasn't playing hide and seek amongst the water reeds, she'd memorized the names of all the garden flowers and tried to pick out which would have been her mother's favorite.

But now she only saw the hunched backs of the gardeners as they baked beneath the too-bright sun. The beauty cultivated for her family and kept from all others. The bright mask that barely concealed the decay underneath.

She was reminded of something Rodrick had asked her once. *'Were you ever truly happy in your palace of sun and slaves, or were you simply blinded by the brightness of it all?'*

The servants did what they did for every pregnant woman of the Sunstar line. They filled her room with broad-leafed tropical plants and opened all the windows. But the windows were still barred, and the plants only served to make Valla's prison more claustrophobic.

Nanook frequently paced at her bedroom door, and Valla often fantasized that she'd open the door and find Rodrick there, smiling down at her. As horrible as she felt for absconding with his favored pet, she was glad to have some piece of the north with her still. Sometimes she woke to Nanook resting her muzzle on her belly and whining softly.

Valla's condition worsened as time passed and the baby grew. She was struck with raging fevers that left her bedridden and weak, her skin icy to the touch. Her very breath could crystallize water, but she felt like she was slowly being baked alive.

During one such bout, Renfrew brought Valla a bowl of medicinal broth. She gagged at the smell of it and hunched over, trying not to vomit. The child was obnoxiously picky in their tastes.

She attempted a sip, then went stumbling for the chamber pot when her stomach flipped. After emptying her guts yet again, she rinsed her mouth of the acidic taste.

Renfrew shook his head and left.

Her temperature continued to plummet as her fever persisted. Renfrew insisted on trying to burn it out. He sent fire mages to fill her room with heat-retaining rocks and braziers that burned cloying medicinal herbs.

Her sisters visited later that day. Valla didn't greet them at the door, too weak to get out of bed. They wore concerned looks when the guards let them in.

"Valla—are you alright?" Eva asked.

"You don't look so good," Cora said. Her youngest sister had grown even taller during Valla's time away. She was beginning to grow into the ornate robes of her station, rather than looking like a child trying on their mother's clothes.

"I feel like death," Valla admitted.

Cora shivered and slid her hands inside the folds of her gown. The room was often cold to others, despite the fire mages' best attempts.

"Is this normal?" Cora asked.

Eva's face pinched. "I don't think so. What the blazes is that doctor doing? I'm going to have one of the harem wet nurses visit. You are clearly unwell—"

"I'm not sure how much they'll know about magical pregnancies."

"Why hasn't the Storm King come for you?" Cora asked.

"He ought to ride down Jotunfjall on his—an *elk*, did you call it? What is that?"

"Picture a very large deer," Eva said.

"Yes. He ought to ride down the mountain on his very large deer and rescue you from father and his fire mages!"

Valla and Eva shared a look. They hadn't told Cora about Valla's letter. She was too young yet to be embroiled in their schemes. They alone would bear the punishment if they were discovered.

"That's only how it goes in story books, I'm afraid," Valla said.

"Well what were the storybooks based on, then?"

Eva sighed wistfully. "Wishes and dreams."

"Other storybooks?" Valla offered. She shifted against her pillows, struggling to get comfortable. "I feel like I'm allergic to this place."

Eva's gaze drifted to the window. "The weather has been... unnatural of late. People are afraid of what it means."

Valla nodded. Her snowy manifestations had grown along with the baby, manifesting in other rooms of the palace and, recently, outside of it.

"I can't control it."

When her sisters had left and Renfrew had come and gone again, Stefan showed up in her rooms. Four of his fire mages accompanied him.

Valla scooted back against the headboard. She would prefer to face them standing, but last time she'd tried to stand up from the bed, her vision had swum and darkened until she sat back down and held her head between her legs.

Nanook blocked Valla with her body and growled at the intruders.

"Why are you here? You need to leave. You're disturbing my rest."

Stefan slipped into his smarmy smile. "Princess. Your little snowstorms are disturbing the citizens. People believe the Storm King is on our doorstep. There is panic in the streets."

"I'm not sure what you expect me to do about it."

"The child needs to be discouraged. Now, are you going to cooperate, or will you need to be restrained?"

"If you harm the baby, my father will have your head."

"I'm quite aware. There will be no lasting damage. Just a little deterrent, for the good of Isaana. You understand."

Valla's eyes darted around the room. His fellow mages wouldn't hesitate to restrain her, which would lead to an even more traumatic experience than whatever Stefan had planned. And however she detested him, his interest in self-preservation exceeded everything else. He wouldn't risk any real harm to the child.

"Fine."

"Bring your mutt to heel."

Valla clenched her teeth. "Let me put her in the hall." She didn't trust Nanook not to go for Stefan's throat, and she couldn't risk the hound's safety.

Valla rose on unsteady feet and tugged Nanook by the scruff toward the door. The massive hound locked her legs, dragging the carpet beneath her paws.

Valla bent down and cupped Nanook's head in her hands. She was teetering on the edge of exhaustion, and tears welled in her eyes.

"Please, girl. I'll be alright. It'll only be a moment."

Nanook relented, letting herself be tugged along by the scruff.

The hound began whining and scratching at the door as soon as it closed between them.

Valla collapsed back on the bed.

"Shirt off," Stefan said.

"What?"

"Shirt off, unless you want me to set your clothes on fire."

Valla rolled her shirt up, exposing her stomach. Her belly had grown enough that she was noticeably pregnant now, even beneath her clothes.

Stefan's fingers grazed the swell of her navel, and Valla's skin began to heat.

The warmth soon turned uncomfortable instead of pleasant, like bare feet on too-hot sand. The baby fluttered restlessly.

Valla's gorge began to rise. Nanook barked outside the door.

Stefan narrowed his eyes, and the heat intensified. His fingers glowed red with power—the color of candlelight shining through flesh.

Valla clenched her teeth as her skin began to scald.

Then she felt a pulse from deep in her core that made her jerk.

Stefan yelped and snatched his hand away, cradling it to his chest. His fingers were blackened at the tips. Had he managed to char himself?

"What the fuck?" he yelled.

Valla frowned at the pink handprint staining her belly. "What happened?"

"You froze my fucking hand! My fingers have frostbite!"

Valla glanced between Stefan and her belly. Sunmother, the child was that powerful, even in the womb?

She cradled her belly and sent her sense of gratitude to the child, hoping they could feel it.

"You failed, Stefan. Now leave me. I need to rest."

CHAPTER 26
RODRICK

With Valla gone, Rodrick buried himself in work. He had her rooms locked up and banned the palace staff from cleaning them. They thought him mad, but he was beyond caring. He was clinging to his last scraps of her like so much melting snow.

Her scent had faded from his furs far too quickly, and with it the light she'd brought to his life. He'd soon descended back into the darkness of his mind.

Astrid tried to pull him out of it, but he fought her every step of the way, and even his oldest friend could only handle so much abuse.

Rough winds battered the keep daily. Servants scattered from his path. Even the council was more bendable than usual.

He'd waited impatiently for word from his Isaanan contact to arrive. Rodrick already planned to go south as soon as spring arrived. He needed to see her—even if from afar, but hopefully a whole lot closer. He missed her touch. Her companionship.

Then Valla's letter had arrived. Rodrick had raged when he

learned she was back in the Sun Palace. He never should have let her leave. He didn't think her longing for freedom had been a ruse. Which meant he had a rat in his court. It wasn't surprising—discontent was bound to flourish during times of hardship.

But he didn't believe for a second that Valla was truly content to be back in her father's grasp. Radagon would not take their failure to marry well.

When Radagon's letter arrived shortly after Valla's, it was brief and to the point:

My daughter carries your spawn, Fjallgard. Come marry her before she whelps, or I will have no further use for her or the child.

Rodrick was tempted to call the Sun King's bluff and show up and abscond with Valla, but he would heed her warning. He couldn't move in any number till spring. He'd have to play his cards carefully in the coming months. He'd posted scouts throughout the tunnels, but little more could be done while he was stuck on the mountain.

Several months after the letters from Sunstone arrived, more disturbing news made its way up Jotunfjall.

Rodrick was deep in his ledgers when Astrid and a foot soldier invaded his office.

Astrid knocked once, then entered without waiting for a response. She perched on the edge of his desk while the soldier twisted his hands in the doorway.

Rodrick didn't look up. "Report."

"We've news of strange weather from the south, sir," the soldier stuttered.

"What sort? Monsoon season come early?"

"Snow, sir."

Rodrick's quill skidded to a stop.

"What did you say?"

"It's snowing in Sunstone."

Rodrick slowly raised his head. There was only one magic strong enough to make it snow so far south, and it ran through his veins. He'd left a kernel of his magic inside Valla so he might find her again if his contact failed to keep tabs on her, but not nearly enough to cause weather phenomena.

"Is this your idea of a joke?"

The pages of his ledger rustled as power pushed at the edges of his control. He'd had to spend more time in his ice garden than ever lately to keep from battering Jotunfjall with storms.

The soldier's eyes went wide and panicky. "No, sire. We've had reports from multiple sources."

Cold dread slid into Rodrick's gut like a knife.

The council elders kept close track of any who bore the frost heart, and Rodrick was the sole carrier this generation. There was no stray cousin causing this.

Which meant his unborn child was making it snow over the Sun Palace.

Fear curdled in the pit of his stomach. The realization ought to have been a joyful one, but it was tainted by his family's history.

Astrid snapped her fingers. "Thank you, soldier. You're dismissed. I'll communicate the particulars."

The soldier gave a sloppy bow and fled.

"Rodrick, I need you to stay calm—"

"What the bloody fuck does it look like I'm doing?"

A sheet of ice now encased his desk. Which he thought was an exceedingly calm reaction, considering.

"If snow falls, that means—"

"Sigurd's beard, I know damn well what it means, Astrid. And you ask me to stay calm?"

"It means she's alive! They both are."

"How? How did this happen? She told me—the blasted

liar. The bloody little fool." He was going to kill her if the frost heart didn't beat him to it.

"We leave tonight."

"You can't. You read her letter. It's not safe to take the tunnels."

"You mean her lies." Her *pretty words*. After everything, she was still lying to him.

How far along was she? He knew the answer. It blared like a siren in his brain. It was a manifestation of his worst fears. Like someone had yanked them from his nightmares into reality.

Six months, since she left. Seven since they first lay together.

Trails of frost began to spread out from his boots, creeping across the room like the doom swallowing his heart.

"My mother didn't survive her fourth month. We cannot wait."

"She's young. Strong."

"The snow—in such a climate—" The snow was a bad sign. It signaled duress, emotional instability.

"She'll be okay, Rodrick."

"She doesn't know! She doesn't know that my mother's pregnancy is how the frost heart killed her. She can't die, Astrid. I won't survive it. Promise me you'll get them out, over everything. Swear it. Swear it to me as your king."

If Valla died, it would be his fault. He never should have risked impregnating her. He'd been a stupid, lust-drunk fool.

"Rodrick Fjallgard, I swear Valla and the child will make it out of this alive. But don't you dare go leaping onto the pyre."

"Prepare the soldiers. You're right, the tunnels are a death trap. We'll take the mountain pass instead, and I'll clear the entire bloody Jotunfjall of snow if I must. We cannot wait for spring thaw. Radagon knows the child has the touch of winter. He'll have Valla under lock and key until the birth."

Astrid nodded. "There's something else you should know."

"Frostmother, what else?"

"Valla asked me about a contraceptive tea after your trip to the flats."

"I'm aware."

"Well, Frieda has always kept meticulous logs of her stores."

"What of it?"

"I checked the logs. There's no entry around that date. And our inventory matches the ledger."

Rodrick shot up from his chair.

"I'm going to kill that wretched hag. Freeze her bit by bit and make her watch me slice pieces off, until there's more of her on the floor than not."

Rodrick stormed out of his office, leaving a black sheet of ice in his wake. A blizzard began to howl outside.

Astrid scurried alongside him, trying not to slip. "Fuckin' icelords," she muttered. "Gonna break my fucking neck."

Rodrick burst into the kitchens, sending the cooks and servants scattering like mice.

"*Frieda!*"

Frieda came out of her office, a serene expression on her face.

"My king. What's wrong?"

A gust of wind blew Frieda against the wall, and shackles of ice grew around her wrists and ankles.

A trickle of fear entered the hearthkeeper's rheumy eyes.

"Rodrick—" Astrid said, reaching out for him.

"*Don't touch me right now. I can't control it.*" His voice throbbed with power. Every breath he took frosted the air.

"Everyone out," Astrid yelled at the servants peeking around doorways at the display.

"Rodrick—" Frieda began.

"*Do not say my name, woman.*"

He was hanging onto his control by a tenuous thread. They needed to get this conversation over with before he made good on his threat to turn her into a slushy.

"What was in the tea blend you gave Valla?"

Frieda's eyes widened and skirted away. "She wanted a contraceptive tea."

"Yes, I'm aware. But what did you actually give her?"

"What are you implying?"

"That you hated the girl from the start because of your prejudices, and you tried to ruin her at every turn."

Frieda's lips twisted together. "We have a limited store of medicinal herbs. They have to last all winter, and more women become sexually active every day. Others cannot afford to bear another bairn."

"Aye, but you don't lie to them about what they're drinking, do you?" Astrid said.

"Why do you care so much about some Isaanan brat who acted above her station?"

The ice spread down Frieda's limbs and up her neck, nearly encasing her entirely. Pebbles of hail began to fall from the ceiling. One plunked into a simmering soup with a sizzle of steam.

"It's none of my concern if she couldn't keep her legs shut. Perhaps she took a souvenir home with her."

Rodrick's voice shook. "What did you do to my wife?"

"*Your wife?*"

"Did you poison her? What the fuck did you give her?"

"It—it was just a bitter tea. Harmless."

Astrid groaned.

Rodrick rippled with rage. "Your hearthkeeper title is revoked. I will personally ensure your name is stricken from the record and reviled in Frostheim. No children shall bear your name for the next one-hundred years. Get off my mountain, and never let me see you again. And believe me, if Valla dies because of your actions, I will hunt you down and make your life an icy hell."

Rodrick strode for the exit and snapped at Astrid to follow. "Leave her to melt."

CHAPTER 27

VALLA

ONE MONTH LATER:

Valla watched from her barred window as winter approached the Sun Palace. Her hand curled over the generous hump of her belly when she spotted Rodrick. Mounted on an enormous white elk, furs doubling the size of his shoulders, he looked every inch a king—proud and furious.

The planes of his cheeks were sharp, and there were shadows beneath his eyes. They'd ridden hard. He'd grown a ragged beard, and his skin was windchapped. Even the usually immaculate Astrid looked worse for the wear.

The child kicked, and frost glazed the bars on her window. Could they sense Rodrick's nearness?

Even if Rodrick had believed her letter, he would know what the Isaanan weather meant. There'd be no hiding the pregnancy from him now. She could only hope that he'd come prepared.

The last few months, the pregnancy had been a beast.

Since entering her third trimester, it snowed more every day, and Valla awoke each morning feeling weaker. Morning sickness and the child's uncontrolled magic had ravaged her. Except for the baby bump, she was sickly thin, almost skeletal. One life source being sucked dry for another.

The longer they'd gone without word from Frostheim, the more her father had raged.

'If he does not come, and you give birth to a useless bastard, I will kill you both. Better yet, I will kill you and raise your son to my side. His power will be his father's downfall.'

She'd heard whispers from the servants. The people were scared—thought the snow was a plague sent from the north to kill the crops. A portent of war.

She'd tried to keep her strength, for the child's sake, but it was like wading through thick water just to get out of bed in the morning. An escape attempt had been far beyond her abilities. But winter had finally come for her.

Rodrick

WHEN RODRICK ARRIVED at the steps of the Sun Palace, he was the only member of his entourage allowed in. He'd expected as much and complied with their demands. He had to cooperate while Valla and his child were held hostage. Rodrick gave a tight nod to Astrid and shouldered past the radiant guards.

When he entered the Sun King's courtroom, Radagon sat atop his gilded throne, the picture of ambivalent luxury.

A servant bent at an awkward angle beside the throne, holding out a platter of fruit within hand's reach.

"Fjallgard. You've finally arrived. Took your time about it. The bitch will whelp soon."

Rodrick tamped down the angry swell of his power. "Where is she?"

The Sun King popped a grape into his mouth, chewing slowly.

"I must say, I wondered what took you so long. But now I realize you were waiting for it to be undeniable that the whelp is yours. Wise. Never trust a woman."

Rodrick's smile was vicious.

Another grape. Radagon spoke as he chewed. "You've come to marry her, then?"

"Why else would winter grace your gates, sun lord? I'm here to take her back home with me."

Radagon's life lifted in a patronizing smirk. "Of course. We will have the wedding tomorrow, with your soldiers as witnesses. Then there can be no doubt as to the child's legitimacy."

Rodrick could feel the flicker of the child's magic nearby. They were close.

"One more thing, son of frost. You may take my daughter back north with you, after she births. But no grandchild of mine will ever see the snow."

Rodrick's mouth slid into a razor smile. "My child *is* the snow. I will see Valla. *Now*."

He had no plans of revealing the frost heart's weakness to Radagon—not unless it was his last option to try and save them. Such knowledge could be used against his people for generations to come.

"Very well. But you will go alone, take no weapons, and I will have a squadron of fire mages posted outside the door. For the baby's safety, you understand."

Rodrick's jaw ticked. "Of course."

Radagon flicked out a hand.

"Stefan, please escort him to Seraphina's chambers."

Stefan? The name tickled at Rodrick's brain. He knew it from somewhere.

When a man in the robes of a high-ranking fire mage approached from behind the king's throne, Rodrick remembered.

The fire mage who'd fucking branded Valla. He'd survived the avalanche?

Four of the radiant guard joined Stefan in escorting Rodrick deeper into the Sun Palace.

"You were on my mountain," Rodrick said. He needed confirmation this was the man. His death would not be a happy one.

"I was."

"You touched her. Scarred her, when she was a *child*."

Stefan scoffed. "Her blood was in. She was woman enough."

An ancient, glacial rage slid through Rodrick. He would bury this palace of greed in rubble. Innocents would die, but that was the cost of war. Of taking, *harming,* what was his.

It was all he could do not to freeze Stefan on the spot. His magic was weaker here, but he could easily summon it for this cretin. The one who'd dared to lay a hand on her—permanently scar her—

He wanted to abandon his magic altogether and wrap his hands around the man's scrawny, tan neck and squeeze until the life left his eyes.

The radiant guards shifted uncomfortably as the temperature began to drop.

"Watch yourself, Fjallgard," Stefan said.

"Likewise, firedog"

Rodrick had to call on discipline earned through years of toil in his ice garden to quell the power sliding through his veins, begging to be unleashed.

They approached a nondescript door deep within the

warren of the Sun Palace. The guards patted him down for weapons once more before gesturing for him to go ahead.

Rodrick took a deep breath to calm himself before stepping inside the room. He could sense the turmoil of the child's magic through the door, and he didn't want to make things worse with his own ragged emotions.

He stepped inside and closed the door behind him.

Valla was pacing back and forth in front of her bed, stirring up snowclouds with every step.

Bone-deep relief filled him. The signs of her being alive had all been there, but he'd needed to see it with his own eyes. That said, she didn't look well.

There was purple bruising beneath her eyes, and she was unnaturally pale. Bone-thin but for the rounded swell of her belly. He blinked at her pregnant stomach—*their child*—and a protective urge swelled within him.

Valla jerked her head up and paused to drink him in, then folded her arms over her chest and resumed pacing.

"You weren't supposed to come."

"A fine welcome after our many months apart."

Rodrick touched the bedroom door and encased it in a sheet of ice to ensure they weren't overheard.

Valla shook her head. "That will not keep the fire mages out."

"It will warn us they are coming."

Nanook stirred from her spot on the bed, then leapt at Rodrick with a happy bark. She braced her paws on his shoulders and tried to lick his face.

Rodrick scratched her ears till her tongue was lolling. "You did a fine job, Nanook. You kept them safe for me." He gave the hound his attention until she calmed down, then turned to back Valla. She was staring out the barred window, a distant look on her face.

His gaze fell to where her hand cradled her stomach.

"Valla, I— Are you okay?"

"As well as can be expected. Your child is...challenging, to say the least."

"Our child."

Her brown eyes softened, and she nodded. "Our child."

He strode toward her, cupped her face in his hands, and ran his thumbs over her cheekbones. They were too sharp— the usual plumpness of her cheeks hollowed out.

He pulled her to him and kissed her like he'd longed to do these past months. She melted in his arms. She was too slight. Too frail. It scared the shit out of him.

His beard rasped against her face. He kissed her deeper, and when he finally pulled back, her face was littered with red striations.

"You self-sacrificing fool. Why'd you lie to me about the pregnancy?"

Valla looked away. "I was trying to save you."

"Losing you is no salvation. You could have died."

His hands skirted down her shoulders to her ribs, then her waist. "Have they harmed you?"

"No. Once they discovered I was pregnant, I became their prize pig. But you aren't safe here, Rodrick—"

"No one is safe here. Least of all you."

"I'm fine."

"You are far from fine, love."

"It's not my fault your child is so damn temperamental."

He bit back a smile. "The child would not be nearly so upset had you stayed where you belonged."

Valla pulled away from him and set her hands on her hips. "And where's that?"

"With me."

She shook her head. "I told you not to come."

He pulled her back against his chest. After so long without

her, he needed to feel her, touch her. Make sure she was actually real. He buried his nose in her hair.

"You don't understand, Valla. It's not just my life at risk here."

"I can handle a little snow. You ought to know that by now."

"You're naught but skin and bone and bruises. The child is draining you dry. I've good as cursed you."

"So you walk right into the trap I told you about?"

"This isn't a regular pregnancy. The danger—" Rodrick paused to steady himself.

"My mother died because she was carrying a child of the frost heart outside Frostheim. My father sent her to another kingdom to tend to negotiations in his stead, but they didn't know she was pregnant. By the time she realized what was happening, it was too late. She couldn't make it back home before the magic drained her. I will not let history repeat itself, even if I have to drag you back up the mountain kicking and screaming."

Valla had the good sense to look afraid.

Rodrick swallowed. "I could kill it. With my magic. It would be painless."

She went still. The temperature in the room started to plummet. "What did you say?"

"It's killing you, Valla. You could have other children, in the future."

She gripped his arms, her nails digging into his biceps. "No! No one is going to hurt our child."

He bowed his head. "I can't lose you. I'd rather have you and no children at all if it means you survive."

Valla picked up his left hand and pulled it to the swell of her navel. "You don't understand. I considered it, at first, but I know them now. I've felt them, these past eight months. The child cannot help it. They are innocent in all this."

Something pushed and fluttered against his palm, and then there was a definite kick. The child's magic pulled at him, sensing its own likeness.

Rodrick sighed and closed his eyes. He'd spent little time entertaining the prospect of fatherhood. He hadn't wanted to get his hopes up. It was easier to handle the potential loss if he thought of the child in abstract terms.

"Very well. But you cannot stay here."

Valla's face fell. "My father will never let us leave. He sees the child as his way to claim the north."

"Aye. He bid us wed tomorrow."

"If you marry me, you sign your death warrant."

"I've got no plans to die yet. We'll figure a way out of this."

Valla's nails dug into his shirt. "How? You can't possibly beat multiple fire mages on their home turf."

Rodrick narrowed his eyes. "With the woman I love and our child at stake? I will bury them in an arctic sea. Impale them on ice spears and feed them to Nanook like kebabs. Freeze all the blood in their veins and unravel them like skeins of yarn."

Wind whipped around them, and a sheet of ice formed around their feet.

Rodrick chuckled and caressed the swell of her belly. "Our child approves. He is powerful."

"Everyone is so sure it's a boy. It could be a girl."

"I would be happy with either, but the frost heart has never passed to a female before."

Valla rolled her eyes. "Misogynistic magic. Lovely."

"Your father bears only daughters. Perhaps the universe has a peculiar way of righting itself."

She rose a single eyebrow. "Cosmic matchmaking, really?"

Rodrick shrugged. "There have been stranger truths." He brushed his hand down her cheek. "We will have daughters, too. He will not be alone."

Her face twisted. "Please. Don't speak of a future you can't ensure."

Valla swayed where she stood, her eyes drifting to the bed. "I don't think they like the south."

Rodrick picked Valla up with ease, one arm behind her back and the other beneath her knees. She was far too light.

"He has no ice garden."

"What?"

"No place to vent his magic. The outbursts are worse when your emotions are running high, yes?"

She nodded.

"He can sense how you're feeling. Your anxiety, your fear. Your anger. The magic is trying to protect itself."

Rodrick carried Valla to the bed and sat with her on his lap. "My father told me of my mother's pregnancy with me. He had to draw off my excess magic as I grew, or it built up to toxic levels in my mother's system. That's why you're suffering. You lack an outlet. The magic is finding ways to manifest regardless, and your body can't handle it. Especially outside Frostheim."

Valla burrowed into him. "It already feels better with you here. I've been so lonely."

"You don't have to be lonely anymore, love. I'm not going anywhere. Tell me what you need."

"I don't know. I feel so hot all the time, but my skin is cold to the touch. And when I get too warm, the nausea sets in." She looked up at him with those big doe eyes. "I never thought I'd long for an ice bath."

He'd chill her bath water until it crackled with cold.

He cast his eyes around the tropical jungle they'd recreated in her room. "It's no wonder. This room is stifling. Fool fire mages trying to sweat out the cold. The baby wants to be in its element. It *needs* the cold. As much as you can stand without your body temperature getting too low."

Rodrick skirted a hand over her belly and sent a small trickle of magic into her skin to see how she reacted.

Valla closed her eyes and moaned, relaxing into him.

"Take off your dress."

She shifted in his lap. "This is hardly the time for—"

He nipped her earlobe. "It will be more effective skin-on-skin. Your clothes are insulating."

"Oh. Right."

Rodrick helped her slide her sleeves off her shoulders and folded her bodice down.

"*Fuck.*" Her breasts were enlarged, preparing for the baby, her blue veins pronounced beneath her skin. Her nipples were duskier than before. He wanted to bite them, to squeeze and lave them until they were stiff against his tongue.

"How I've ached for you."

"Have you—" Her throat bobbed when she swallowed. "Have you been with another? Since I left?"

"No, Valla. You're the only one I want."

He slid his fingers along her collarbone. It protruded too sharply against the skin. All the nutrients in her body were going to support the child.

Valla looked down, following his gaze. "My body is different."

"You're gorgeous. But you need to eat more."

Valla snorted. "Tell that to your child. I've thrown up more meals than not since the start of this."

Rodrick smirked. "Perhaps they don't like what you're feeding them. Have you tried any of my favorites?"

Valla groaned, and Rodrick chuckled.

"The trouble that comes of trying to drag winter into the sun."

"More like your child's an ornery bastard."

"He will not be a bastard."

She stiffened in his arms again and wouldn't meet his gaze. He traced lines of frost over her womb, trying to soothe her.

"Did you come for me, or the child?"

"I'm here for both of you, Valla."

"But without the child, you wouldn't be here right now. I want them to know you, but I don't want to be together just for the child's sake."

Her breath hitched, and tears streaked down her face.

Rodrick wiped them away with his thumbs. Ice pierced his chest. "I have been miserable without you. You are everything I've ever wanted. Ever needed. If I could, I would move to this wretched, sun-soaked place and let its rays ravage me for you."

Valla choked on a sob. She threw her arms around him and began weeping into his neck.

He rubbed his hands up and down her back. "What is it, little flower? What's wrong?"

"What are we going to do?"

"We will marry."

She shoved away from him. "We will do no such thing."

"My hand in marriage is the best protection I can give you both. Don't worry. If it's the last thing I do, I'll get you out of here."

"It will *not* be the last thing you do, you stubborn man. I can't do this without you. You should never have come—"

He fixed his hands on her shoulders. "Valla, the likelihood of you surviving the entire pregnancy in this clime—I don't think it's possible. You're already skin and bones. There is an inch of snow sticking to the sand a mile outside the palace. It will only get worse, and you don't have much left to give. I won't lose another woman I love to this curse. I will not lose you again."

"My father will never let us be happy."

"Do you not believe I can keep you safe from him?"

"It's not me I'm worried about. If I lose you, my heart will never be whole again.

Something squeezed inside Rodrick's chest. "Everything will be alright. You need to rest. Tomorrow will be taxing."

They lay together in bed, Rodrick cradling her from behind. He traced his hand over her belly, over and over again, sending tiny trickles of frost across her skin when the baby began to stir. Rodrick weaved layers of cold magic over her body, building it slowly, until the baby's magic hummed peacefully and Valla was asleep in his arms.

CHAPTER 28

VALLA

On the day of her wedding, Valla awoke feeling more refreshed than she had in months.

She'd dozed in Rodrick's arms all night as he'd whispered sweet nothings to her. How beautiful she looked swollen with his child. How he longed to see her wrapped in his furs again. How he missed the glow of her hair lit by his fireplace. How she was a sun maiden sent to bring light to his life.

Among his platitudes were not *I love you*, but she didn't fault him for it. Their current relationship was built on circumstance. Who knows if they'd have ever seen each other again without her capture or the child. There would be time enough to figure out what they were to one another once they made it out of their current mess.

The wedding preparations were rushed and cobbled together, but grand enough that her father must have begun planning as soon as reports of Rodrick's descent from Jotunfjall arrived. Valla wasn't consulted on any of it. It was her father's show, and she had a bit part to play.

She and Rodrick didn't partake in the traditional pre-wedding rituals, as Rodrick refused to leave her side. She did not miss them. It was not going to be the wedding of her dreams, but then, she'd never had many to begin with.

Valla's sisters styled her hair for her. Radagon had his seamstress tailor a golden gown in thick brocade to fit her new waistline. The fabric was stifling and weighed down with jewels. She felt like an ornament as she clinked up the steps to the throneroom alongside Rodrick.

The Storm King wore his furs and an antlered headpiece that made him look like a creature out of myth.

The throneroom was decorated in red and gold finery—her father's colors. The servants must have been working round the clock to get everything prepared in time.

The audience was split by faction. The right side of the room bristled with high-ranking Isaanan nobles, advisors, and guards. The left of the aisle hosted a smaller contingent of Frostheimers, easily identified by their pale hair and skin. There weren't enough Frostheimers present to fill the entire half of the room, and some wedding planner had clearly grabbed people from the streets to fill the last quarter of the seats.

As they began the long approach to the dais together, Valla balked.

Stefan stood at the end of the aisle, his robes even gaudier than usual. It was tradition for a high-ranking fire mage to officiate an Isaanan handfasting of this caliber, but she hadn't expected him.

Rodrick tensed beside her.

"That's Stefan," Valla said.

"I'm aware. He will not wed us."

"It's okay—"

Rodrick's magic sparked against her skin.

"No, it isn't. Your father is very close to getting what he

wants. He has never been easier to manipulate than in this moment."

Rodrick rose his voice loud enough to be heard across the room. "I want a different officiant."

The crowd bristled. Stefan wore a bored expression. Radagon sighed.

"Why? He is one of my finest mages—"

"And a coward who abandoned your daughter to the Jotunfjall. One you let mark her flesh."

Valla stiffened as the crowd began to whisper among themselves. Her fingers dug into Rodrick's muscular forearm. What was he doing?

Radagon gestured, and another fire mage approached from the crowd.

"No. No fire mages. This will be done in the northern tradition. My shieldmaiden will officiate."

Radagon's cheeks flushed. He tapped the arms of his chair, then waved his hand. "Fine. Get on with it."

Astrid appeared from the crowd and took up Stefan's spot at the end of the aisle.

Valla's shoulders relaxed. Though a farce, this moment carried a certain kind of magic, and she didn't want her memories of it marred by Stefan's presence.

The walk down the long aisle to Astrid passed in a blink. Then they were standing in front of her, Astrid's words buzzing in Valla's ears.

Valla felt the swell of nausea that accompanied the baby's magical outbursts and shot Rodrick a frantic glance.

He took her hand and squeezed it, letting his magic flow into her.

How much power did he have to spare, in the heart of the sun? He wouldn't be able to recharge like he normally did, and he'd spent all night pumping cold into her. It was the first dreamless, peaceful sleep she'd had since exiting the tunnels.

The adoring expression on Rodrick's face cut her like a knife. How much longer would she have him? She wasn't ready to let him go.

Astrid quieted.

"It's time for the vows, Valla," Rodrick said, and his voice drug her back.

He turned to face her and stroked a thumb down her cheek. He spoke loud enough for everyone in the room to hear. She'd never felt so exposed.

"I want you as my wife. As the mother of my children."

There was muffled tittering from the crowd.

"As my *queen*. But I will take you any way I can have you. You are mine, Seraphina Sunstar. Body and soul. You carry a piece of me inside you now. You are my sun in winter, and I will follow you over any horizon."

Valla squeezed his fingers hard enough to bruise. Tears welled in her eyes.

She hadn't prepared anything, so she spoke from the heart.

"Rodrick Fjallgard. I am winter's prisoner now, because I am yours. Body and soul. But I am learning to love the cold."

Rodrick's heart bled from his eyes as he smiled at her.

Astrid tied a silk ribbon around their wrists.

"Alright. In the eyes of the Frostmother, sun goddess, whoever you worship—you two are wed. Especially as you've already handled the consummation."

Rodrick pulled Valla close and kissed her. It was swift and fierce, but not near long enough to be their last. As their lips parted, he whispered, "Don't try to be a hero, wife."

"What?"

Rodrick slipped his hand free of their ribbon and pulled away. Cries began to ring out around them.

Valla's heart leapt. It'd been foolish, to think he'd show up without a plan. But why hadn't he warned her?

The different halves of the room were standing now, weapons drawn.

Someone swung, and chaos erupted.

Rodrick pulled a sword from the sheath on Astrid's belt and strode into the fray.

Valla stood there, ribbon dangling from her wrist. More members of the radiant guard rushed into the room. Crimson-robed fire mages began to lob balls of crackling flame.

Valla was frozen in place. She felt like she was moving through mud—everything happening slowly, then all at once.

Astrid tugged at her arm. "Come on, princess."

"Help him. Please. They won't hurt me."

"My job is getting you to safety. Your presence here will distract Rodrick—"

Astrid ducked low, narrowly dodging the swing of a radiant guard's shining sword.

Valla hadn't even seen him approach.

Astrid pulled her weapon and turned just in time to parry the guard's next swing.

"Go, Valla! Find somewhere safe to hide, and we'll find you after."

Hide? She couldn't *hide,* waiting to find out who would come to collect her. Who would survive the bloodbath.

Her stomach roiled, and she glanced down. The baby. Fuck. Astrid was right; she would only serve as a distraction here.

Valla glanced around, then scrambled up the steps towards the throne. The regular exits were blocked by the press of bodies as civilians struggled over one another to escape and more of the radiant guard tried to enter. But there was a hidden exit behind the throne that her father used.

She heard Rodrick's yell and swung her head back, frantically searching the crowd for him. A large spear of ice jettisoned across the red aisle runner, directly toward Stefan.

Stefan waved his arm, and the spear melted into a puddle of water.

Smoke began to fill the room as one of the wall hangings bearing her father's insignia caught on fire, real flames eating away at the stitched ones.

Cries of pain and rage rung out. Valla's stomach kicked and rolled. Her panic was affecting the baby.

She took several quick, sharp breaths. She couldn't lose it. She had to remain calm—

Someone wrenched her by the hair, yanking out her bridal headpiece and pulling her against them.

"More trouble than they're worth, daughters," Radagon hissed in her ear.

"What are you doing? Let me go!"

Valla struggled in his grip. The roots of her hair were on fire.

"Ensuring I'm not cheated of what's rightfully mine. Your mother was a deceitful whore too, you know. She begged so loudly when she died. *Weak*. You're all *weak*."

Radagon began marching her towards the throne.

Valla wanted to scream for help, but she clamped her mouth shut. Rodrick and Stefan were flinging spells at one another faster than her eye could track. It was a blur of frost and fire. Stefan had the advantage here, in this monument to the sun. One moment of distraction, and Rodrick would be engulfed by flames.

Radagon yanked harder, and Valla bit her cheek as tears welled in her eyes. She stumbled after him, trying to relieve the pressure on her skull.

"You will hurt the baby!"

"I would sooner cut the babe from your belly than let that heathen take my throne."

It was impossible to tell who was winning the fight amid the fiery pandemonium, but one thing was clear—Rodrick was outnumbered. He was one battlemage against many. Already, several people were shrieking as flames found their flesh. It wasn't a fair fight. The Frostheimers would die trying to free her, and it'd be all her fault.

Ice began to coil in her belly and throat.

Radagon reached beneath his throne's cushioned seat and pulled out a dagger.

Valla twisted away and clawed at his grip on her hair. She wanted to rip free, but she was too weak, the pain too overwhelming.

A Frostheim battlecry went up at the entrance to the throneroom. More soldiers in northern gear poured in, armed to the teeth. Where had they come from?

Valla saw silver flashing toward her and acted on instinct. She caught the dagger in her hand. It sliced deep into her palm, and this time she couldn't hold in her scream.

Blood began to pour from the wound. Radagon wrenched the dagger back to swing again.

Thunder cracked inside the throne room. The chandeliers began to swing wildly.

Power boiled inside her as her vision whited out.

Then it erupted out from her like steam from a geyser

A sheet of white blanketed the throne room.

Her father froze in place, one of his hands still buried in the bodice of her gown.

His eyes were glassed over, his skin caked in frost. His mouth frozen in a scream.

Valla tugged away from him, but his grip on her gown was stiff.

She pulled again. There were several sharp cracks as she broke free.

The din of the fighting rung in her ears. The stench of smoke and magic clogged the air.

Valla slumped toward the floor, utterly drained. The baby

kicked and elbowed at the walls of her stomach. She drug her bloody palm to her belly and stroked, trying to calm them. That pulse of power had been significant.

There was a large crack, and her father's face fractured. His sneer splintered like shattered glass, the fissures spreading faster and faster across his skin.

Valla didn't understand what was happening. Radagon began to tip forward, and she scrambled away.

He toppled to the floor like a felled statue and exploded across the sunbaked tile. Chunks of red ice skidded across the floor. Like a glacier of blood rupturing. There was...meat. Pieces of her father.

Valla blinked, then forced herself to look away.

She searched the throng for Rodrick. He was still locked in combat with Stefan, using columns to dodge the fire now rather than defusing it with his powers.

The pieces of her father started to melt. More rapidly than ice usually melted, as if the magic could only hold on so long. A pool of blood spread across the tile toward her. Valla scrambled backwards, searching for someone, anyone—

She had no love lost for her father, but seeing him *unmade* by her hand shook her to her core. Like she'd knocked off his crown and found it was the only thing holding together the rot underneath.

Cries of "The king is dead!" began to go up around her.

People turned and looked. At her. At the destruction she'd caused.

Rodrick whipped around. His face went white with dread.

A wave of fire roared toward his back.

But he wasn't looking. He was staring at the pile of meat formerly known as Radagon, then up at her, not paying attention—

"Watch out!" Valla screamed. He swung back around, but it was too late.

The fire vanished inches from Rodrick's face.

Valla frantically searched for Stefan in the crowd.

She spotted him by a charred tapestry. A spear stuck out of his chest. He clutched at it as blood dribbled from his mouth.

Astrid raised her boot and kicked Stefan off her spear, then sunk the tip into his throat. The fire mage slumped to the ground, lifeless.

"Isaana! Cease fighting if you wish to live!" Astrid roared. "Your king is dead."

A giant cramp hit Valla's abdomen, and she clutched her belly and leaned forward, curling into a tight ball.

Something wet slipped between her thighs. She ripped at her skirts and pushed her hand between her legs. It came away covered in blood.

"Valla!"

Her name came from a million miles away. The knot of pain in her belly clenched tighter, and she fell to the floor as darkness washed across her vision.

CHAPTER 29
VALLA

Valla came to beneath the floral pattern of her childhood bedroom yet again. She felt like a well-used rag that'd been thoroughly wrung out. She would've thought the last twenty-four hours a mad dream if not for the absence of the scent of burning herbs.

Rodrick sat folded in half beside the bed, his head cradled in his hands.

Valla tried to sit up and groaned. Nanook began to bark.

Rodrick lifted his head. "You're awake. Thank fuck."

He looked done in. Like he hadn't slept in days and was on the verge of collapsing.

Valla rubbed her temples, trying to dispel the fog in her head. "Is everyone okay? What happened?"

Rodrick nodded. "Your sisters and Astrid are fine. There were some unavoidable casualties, but things have calmed down. The fire mages may give us some trouble, but everyone else was eager enough to lay down weapons once they realized they weren't sure who they were fighting for anymore. I have forces stationed throughout the keep and the city while things settle."

Valla pushed at Rodrick's chest, too weak to do much else. "You didn't warn me."

"I know. I couldn't risk you playing at hero, darling. I needed you surprised, not trying to intervene. I was still evaluating the situation when we entered the throne room. My vows contained a signal for my people to act or not."

Valla's gaze fell. "Oh." All she heard was that he didn't trust her, that everything had been manufactured without her knowledge.

Rodrick squeezed her hand. "Don't give me that look. I meant every word, wife."

Wife. That's right. She was married to the Storm King of Frostheim.

Valla glanced down at the sheet pulled up to her waist. She focused in until she felt the faint buzz of the child's magic in her belly, then let out a sigh of relief.

She grabbed Rodrick's hand and pulled it to her navel. "The baby. I feel them."

"Aye. They're alright, love."

Someone cleared their throat from the corner of the room, and Valla looked over. A plump woman with wispy white hair and the muted garb of Frostheim stood there, hands tucked into the pockets of her brown dress. She looked vaguely familiar.

Rodrick gestured to the woman. "This is Aslog. She's a midwife from Frostheim. She arrived this morning, with the rest of my soldiers."

Aslog approached the bedside. "Don't be modest, cherub. I was the first to see him greet the world, 'twixt his mother's thighs."

"Aslog oversaw my mother's pregnancy with me. She's experienced with the dangers of a magical pregnancy. I trust her with your care."

"What do you think of all this?" Valla asked her.

"Well, you shouldn't be alive still, 'tis the long and short of it. Didn't believe Rodrick when he told me how far along you were. Frankly, it's a miracle you've survived this long. We lost the king's mother around the third month mark."

Valla swallowed. "Is the baby okay? Why did I bleed?"

"The bleeding was a result of stress and strenuous activity. Namely, the magical outburst you experienced."

Right. She'd killed her father. Valla was too numb to process her feelings about it right now. It'd been more a defensive reaction than anything intentional. She hadn't even consciously controlled the magic.

Rodrick nodded. "That surge of power—fuck, Valla, I've never felt anything like it.

"Our child is powerful," Valla said, rubbing her stomach.

Aslog nodded, and Valla turned to her. "Be straight with me. Will the baby survive? Will I?"

Rodrick's hand tightened around hers.

"If you hope to, the child needs to be born in the north, where his power is strongest. After the stress and excitement of the wedding—not to mention the magical outpouring felt a mile way—I would not be at all surprised if the baby comes early. He is agitated. Your condition is deteriorating daily. You need to leave as soon as you're able. You should have left days ago."

Rodrick glanced between Aslog and Valla. "She can't ascend the mountain in her condition. The tunnels are too steep, and she'll never make it back up the pass in snow that thick.

"Then you should get as close to Jotunfjall as possible. Proximity is important. Rodrick, your powers will be essential for keeping the birthing environment cold."

Rodrick nodded. His face was grave, his grip on Valla's hand tight enough to bruise.

"We'll leave as soon as you've recovered enough to travel."

. . .

POLITICAL MATTERS also had to be handled before they left for Frostheim. The Sun Palace was in disorder following the havoc of the wedding and Radagon's death. There were several meetings hosted in Valla's bedchamber, since Rodrick was tyrannical about her bedrest.

Radagon hadn't formally named an heir, so succession defaulted to the family line. Valla abdicated her responsibilities to Evangeline, her younger sister. Eva had a better head for politics, and Valla could hardly rule effectively from Frostheim —plus she wasn't going to be separated from Rodrick and their child. Truthfully, she had little desire to rule. She was much more interested in discovering the other things life had to offer.

When they finally packed up and headed back north, Valla set the pace. Their progress was slow. The baby's magical outbursts were increasing in frequency, and a trail of frost accompanied their entourage. Rodrick did his best to siphon the child's energy and calm them with his magic, but he was looking more haggard by the day. He hadn't had a chance to recharge since the wedding battle.

Rodrick laid with her in their tent each night and traced patterns of frost over her belly. He'd whisper to the babe, and the reassuring cool of his magic would lull her to sleep.

Valla's contractions began as soon as they reached the base of Jotunfjall. As if the baby couldn't wait any longer, now that they were so close.

They made camp on a patch of farmland at the foot of Jorumungar's Pass. The landowners, an elderly farmer and his wife, were given plenty of coin for their trouble.

Valla was set up in an old cabin—the closest readily available structure to the mountain.

The place was dusty and ill-kempt. With the war on, it'd

been long out of use. Still, Rodrick's soldiers had it spick and span within a matter of hours.

Valla was growing increasingly worried as her contractions progressed. The baby was coming three weeks early.

"Is it going to be okay? If I give birth here?" she asked Aslog.

The midwife wore a calm, kind expression. It was a welcome change from the anxiety Rodrick was exuding from every pore.

"These are unprecedented circumstances, Valla. The baby is strong. Rodrick has felt their magic. He's mimicking Frostheim's environment as best he's able. The conditions are as ideal as we can make them."

"Everything is going to be okay," Rodrick said. "You can do this."

Rodrick had turned the cabin into a veritable igloo. A blizzard whipped outside the thin cabin walls throughout Valla's labor. There was no calming the baby now—they wanted *out*.

Birth proved to be a bloody affair. By the end of it, she was cursing Rodrick's name, cock, and cum, and swearing that they were never having sex again.

Rodrick held Valla's hand and wiped her brow through the entire thing. Until his hand was numb and bloodless and he could hardly hold himself up from all the magic he was pumping into the room.

When the child finally slipped free, Valla collapsed back against the bed, panting. Rodrick whispered reassurances against her sweaty forehead and pressed his lips to her brow. Valla was exhausted, but she needed to see the child. She felt their loss keenly after being together for so many months.

Aslog wrapped the baby in a fur and passed them into Rodrick's arms.

Rodrick blinked down, stunned.

"What? What is it?" Valla's heart began to race. Was something wrong?

"It's a girl."

Rodrick stepped toward Valla and lowered the tiny, mewling bundle into her arms. Her daughter's face was wrinkly and red, and she had a thick crown of Valla's dark hair.

Rodrick bent to kiss Valla and traced a finger along his daughter's cheek.

"I've never seen anything so beautiful."

"A girl," Valla said.

The child stared up at them with wide silver eyes, eager to greet the world. They sparked with the familiar electricity of Rodrick's magic.

"She has your eyes."

"She's a good weight, despite being early," Aslog said. "Pink and lively. She'll be a right terror. Now, I'm going to check that you two haven't buried the entire valley in snow."

Rodrick caressed his daughter's head. "What shall we name her?"

Valla smiled up at her husband. "We'll come up with something together. Something new."

CHAPTER 30
VALLA

They named her Brenna.

Once Valla and the baby recovered from the birth, their party continued north. Valla and Rodrick were eager to get Brenna up the mountain. There'd been no magical outbursts since the delivery, but it was only a matter of time, and they couldn't risk the frost heart's curse affecting her.

Astrid, bless her soul, had rounded up some of the more amenable fire mages from Sunstone and brought them north to melt the snow still coating Jorumungar's Pass. It eased their ascent considerably.

When Brenna wasn't glued to Valla's tit, she rode on Rodrick's chest in a sling wrapped around his body, bundled up in a fur trimmed down to her size.

Valla worried about the cold at first, but her daughter came alive on the mountain. Her eyes were bright and curious, even when her nose and cheeks went pink with winter's chill. She slept soundly most nights. Nanook had chosen Brenna as her new charge, and the hound slept curled around the baby's bassinet as snowflakes drizzled onto its canopy.

Valla squeezed Rodrick's hand tight as they gazed at their sleeping daughter, enraptured.

"She's so fucking adorable. It hurts my heart to look at her," Rodrick said.

"I think that's called love, dear."

"I do. I love her so much it frightens me."

A FEW DAYS into their return to the keep, Brenna was down for a nap, so Valla went for a stroll in Rodrick's ice garden.

She stilled when she stepped through the doors to the snowy clearing. A new sculpture knelt at the side of the lake, its hand trailing through the frozen water. The carvings that'd been here before were gone, though some evidence of them remained. Shattered pieces of ice were scattered across the lake surface. Rodrick had destroyed them.

The new sculpture had a woman's shape. Intricate curls fluttered around its hooded face. A long cloak trailed behind her, the folds of fabric wrinkled and pooling atop the snow. It was some of Rodrick's best work. Hyper realistic, as if the woman was a second from standing and turning to face her with a smile.

Valla moved closer, walking across the frozen lake until she was close enough to peek beneath the woman's hood.

Her heart thudded in her chest when she recognized her own face staring back at her. The statue's expression was forlorn and worried as she gazed past the water's surface. Valla's heart wrenched. Why had Rodrick created this, after she'd left him?

Valla moved deeper within the garden. An icen winter elk stepped out from a crystal forest, frozen mid-stride. Another figure with her likeness sat atop it, hands knotted in the thick fur at the elk's neck. The carving wore an expression of trepidatious excitement.

Valla broke into a jog, moving deeper within the garden. She found an ice carving of herself staring at the sky, laying beneath a pile of furs. Then completely nude, her hair twisting wild in the wind. The brand on her hip was absent, and her hands cradled a stomach swollen with child.

Valla's throat went jagged.

And then, at the end of the garden path, a lone bench sat. Her likeness sat on one end of it, left arm cradling a swaddled babe, the other propping open a book. Valla's sculpted face was focused on the child, as if she'd been interrupted midsentence.

The seat beside the statue on the bench was clear of snow. And below, two deep hollows in the shape of boot prints slowly filled with snowfall.

A stone rose in Valla's throat. They were beautiful, and she hated them. They were monuments to Rodrick's pain. To the gaping hole her absence had left.

Snow crunched behind her. She'd recognize the weight of his muffled footsteps on snow anywhere.

"Rodrick." Her voice broke.

Her husband walked up behind her and wrapped his arms around her abdomen, then buried his face in her hair.

"Why?" she asked.

"I missed you, princess."

Her tears were hot against her snow-kissed cheeks. Her shoulders began to shake.

He spun her around and ran a thumb beneath her eyes, catching the fresh tears. "Don't cry, darling. There have been enough tears shed in this garden."

"I don't understand."

"I would have you with me, in one form or another."

"They're beautiful, Rodrick, but—"

"I know."

In his sculptures he'd captured his sadness and longing. His rage.

Beads of water slid down the sculpture's face, dripping into her lap like tears.

She glanced up at Rodrick. "What's happening?"

"I don't need them anymore, Valla. I have the real thing."

Rodrick waved his hand, and all of the statues began to rapidly melt, dripping out of existence.

Valla hated to see his work destroyed, but she recognized that they were painful reminders for him.

"I love you, Valla Fjallgard. I think I have for a long, long time."

Valla twisted her hands around his neck and pulled him close for a kiss.

"I love you, too. I never want to make you sad again."

Rodrick pulled her close and rested his head on hers.

"They made for poor company anyway. Not nearly as talkative as the real thing. We'll make a new garden. Together."

Valla smiled up at him. "I suppose Brenna's going to need room to work."

He slid his thumb below her chin and lifted her head. "There's something I've been meaning to ask you, wife. I didn't get to do it properly before."

"What is it?"

"Will you marry me?"

"Always."

EPILOGUE
RODRICK

R odrick was buried in the minutiae of kingship in his office, counting the minutes until he was done and could go be with his wife and daughter. After their hurried exit from Sunstone, Valla's middle sister, Evangeline, had been formally crowned Queen of Isaana. She was the first Sun Queen in a century.

Rodrick and Valla kept in frequent contact with her. They traveled down the mountain at least once a year so his wife and daughter could spend time with family and Brenna could learn about the other half of her heritage.

Evangeline had upheld Radagon's original marriage treaty, plus some, gifting Frostheim a large plot of arable land at the base of Jotunfjall. The cottage Valla had given birth in now belonged to them, and the elderly couple who'd owned the farm were enjoying their twilight years by the seashore.

The new queen was making moves to improve conditions in Isaana. She'd freed the women in Radagon's harem, offering them enough coin to get established elsewhere or jobs in the palace, whatever they wished. She was working to repeal the harshest of her father's laws and reform their more brutal customs, but progress was slow, and the upper class wasn't going without a fight.

Astrid—a newly promoted member of Rodrick's council —had begun a program that incentivized Frostheimers to move south and develop the new land. Old prejudices died hard, and the interweaving of their two peoples would move slowly, but Rodrick hoped to see progress in his lifetime.

Rodrick had begun construction on a new, smaller keep at the base of the mountain, so that his family and his people might still enjoy summer's warmth. It was a symbolic move, too. A bringing of their peoples closer together. He was determined not to repeat his great-uncle's mistakes.

There was a knock at his door. Rodrick glanced out his office window and sighed. The sun was already setting.

He leaned back in his chair and rubbed at his eyes. "Come in," he grunted.

Valla swept inside, leading Brenna by the hand. Nanook trotted after, nosing at Brenna's skirts. The hound had taken to the girl like shine on an apple, and never let her out of her sight. She was growing old in the muzzle, but was still fiercely protective.

Rodrick smiled at the two most important women in his life and set down his quill. His daughter had grown into quite the little menace. She had her run of the keep and was skilled at charming its denizens into spoiling her rotten.

"Your daughter has something she'd like to show you," Valla said.

"Oh? What's that?"

Brenna crawled into his lap, and Rodrick bounced her on his knee. She was growing up far too quickly. It seemed like just yesterday she was still crawling about his furs on her belly and teething on sanded antlers.

"Show him," Valla whispered.

"I can only do it when I'm mad!"

Valla tickled Brenna's ribs. "Trust me, snowflake, you can do it even when cook isn't denying you a third creampuff."

"Do what?" Rodrick asked.

"Just watch."

Brenna wriggled in his lap and tensed all her muscles. She closed her eyes and furrowed her brow. He was familiar with this expression from her diaper-wearing days, and he shot Valla a baleful look.

Valla began to laugh, and Brenna yelled, "Not funny!"

The letter he'd been writing burst into flames.

Valla picked Brenna up beneath her arms and swung her around.

"Well done, darling!"

"What the—"

"Fire!" Brenna shrieked.

Rodrick quickly doused the flaming parchment with a bit of frost before the flames could spread.

Brenna poked out her lower lip in a pout. "Daddy! No fair."

Valla wore a sly grin. "There have been a few instances, but we weren't sure—then she set cook's apron on fire today."

Rodrick stilled. There was no doubt his daughter had inherited the frost heart. The magical outbursts when her emotions ran high had continued after the pregnancy. Rodrick had calmed more than one of the storms her tantrums kicked up. When she was still nursing, there'd been an incident with a frozen nipple or two that sent Valla yelping. And lately, when a boy teased Brenna or she grew frustrated with her lessons, she'd turn the classroom into a snowy, knee-deep playground for all the children.

She was known in the keep as the Storm Princess, and she'd earned her right to the name.

"It's not possible." Fire and frost did not play well together.

Valla rolled her eyes. "Obviously, it is."

Rodrick looked down at his daughter and swallowed. If she'd inherited both the frost heart and the flame powers of the Isaanan fire mages, she would be a formidable force. And a target.

She'd also need training—and soon. The classroom would not fare half so well when she lit someone's desk on fire.

THAT NIGHT IN BED, with Brenna curled up with Nanook in Valla's old rooms, his wife turned to him.

"You know what this could mean."

Fear slithered down his spine. His daughter was such a pure light in this harsh world. Seeing it quenched would be his undoing.

"We can't risk it."

"The signs have always been there. When we travel south and you begin to weaken, she shows no signs of it. The pregnancy—"

"You nearly died!"

"But I didn't. And I was in Isaana almost the entire time. We'll be careful, Rodrick. But we need to know. For all our sakes."

He sighed. "I don't like it."

"What are you so afraid of?"

There was a small kernel of fear that if their theory were right, Brenna and Valla would abandon the mountain and never return. "Turning into my great-uncle. The two of you leaving me. Not being able to chase after you."

Valla snuggled closer to him.

"She is light *and* snow. The north is in her blood. She will not abandon it. And I've grown rather attached to you, personally."

"Have you now?"

They tested their theory slowly—painfully slowly. They took time away from court to spend in their cabin at the base of the mountain. Close enough that they could find the snow again quickly, if something went wrong.

When Rodrick began to feel the effects of his time away, they kept a watchful eye on Brenna. They monitored her for fatigue, temperature sensitivity, or feelings of weakness.

They increased her time away from the north little by little, but her energy never flagged. Even when Rodrick was on his last leg and Valla was screaming at him to get his ass back up the mountain.

With more time spent in Isaana, Brenna's fire powers were beginning to flourish—the manifestations now coming as frequently as her ice magic. Rodrick's reflexes were tested by the amount of things she accidentally set aflame, and he vowed to begin training her in control and emotional modulation when they returned home, lest she light her next governess on fire.

Eventually, there was no denying it—his daughter was not bound by the same magic that tethered him. She was free.

Valla was giddy. Rodrick was terrified. That she'd leave him, that they'd somehow gotten it wrong, and with enough time outside Frostheim, Brenna would simply fade into snowfall and blow away in the wind.

One night when he and Valla were lying naked in bed, Rodrick's doubts were plaguing him hard.

"I've been wanting to ask you a question," Valla said.

Rodrick swallowed. Here it was. He'd been waiting for it —the inevitable. Valla had been trapped at his side by circumstance since the beginning, but with Radagon gone and

Brenna free to live wherever she wished, they were no longer tethered to his side.

He closed his eyes. "I know."

Panic roiled in his chest, and the temperature in the room began to drop. The hearthfire shrank down as it struggled to stay lit.

"Rodrick, what is it? What's wrong?" She was familiar with all his tells by now.

He forced the words out. "With Brenna free—truly free—I knew you might want to leave." His chest felt tight, and he had to swallow past the thick thing in his throat before speaking again. "I can't lose you. But I will not cage you, either."

Valla rolled on top of him and straddled his hips. It was testament to the extent of his inner turmoil that his cock didn't immediately stir in interest.

"Open your eyes."

He shook his head.

"Please open your eyes, husband."

"Not fair," he muttered, obeying. She was resplendent. Dark curls dangling over his chest. A smile curving her lips. He bit back a groan when she swiveled her naked hips atop his.

"You're a fool, Rodrick Fjallgard."

She adjusted herself so that the head of his cock slipped between her wet folds, then slid her hips forward.

Rodrick gripped her upper thighs. If she continued like that, he wouldn't be able to resist fucking her.

"I love you. I'm not going anywhere without you. Nor is Brenna—at least not for a long, long time."

Valla ground herself against him, her chest flushing red. He'd hardened quickly, and he was beginning to leak precum onto his abdomen. His fingers dug into her.

"What was your question, *witch*?"

"I was going to ask," she began, pausing as she made

another languorous slide of her drenched pussy against him. "If you wanted to make another baby."

That got his attention.

"What?"

"I stopped taking my contraceptive today. Now that it's clear that they'd be safe. That they'd have options."

Rodrick groaned. The thought of pumping another child into his little temptress of a wife—watching her swell with it, and being there for every second of the pregnancy, this time—was enough to nearly send him over the edge. He'd been robbed of the chance to spoil her when she was pregnant with Brenna. To tend to her every need, wait on her hand and foot, and make love to her while she was heavy with his child. Rough, slow—however she needed it.

Valla bit her lip as she shuddered against him. Her juices were spread all over his abs. "I want another one."

Rodrick lifted her hips and repositioned his cock, then lowered her atop him. He slid into her, and Valla tossed her head back and started to ride.

His fingers dug into the area where her ass met her thighs, willing himself not to come as she tightened around him.

"Yes."

"Yes?"

"Yes, I want to put another baby in you. I'm going to fuck you senseless, princess."

He fingered her clit, and Valla moaned with each delicious slide up and down his cock.

"Going to fill you up so much—you'll never get rid of me."

AUTHOR'S NOTE

Love it or hate it or somewhere in between, it'd be great if you could leave me a review. Reviews are the lifeblood of authors like me, and they allow me to keep writing. Thank you!

You can sign up for my newsletter at **sarasellers.com** for exclusive content, cover reveals, release alerts, and more.

ADVANCED READER TEAM

Want to be part of my advanced reader team that receives early access to new releases?

Sign up at **sarasellers.com/links**

Acknowledgments

Thanks to everyone who has read my books and encourages me to keep writing, even when it's hard. Thank you also to my cats, my Baratza Encore, and my wrists, for hanging in there.

About the Author

Sara Sellers writes fast-paced fantasy romance full of action, angst, and the tropes you love.

She lives in middle-of-nowhere, Georgia with her three cats. She likes the sound of rain, the smell of gasoline, and the taste of boiled peanuts. She's an avid gamer and loves a good training montage. She can often be found inside, coffee in hand and YouTube ambiance video on in the background.

Find out more at www.sarasellers.com

tiktok.com/@sellerssara

facebook.com/authorsarasellers

x.com/sellerssara

instagram.com/sellerssara

pinterest.com/sellerssara

goodreads.com/sarasellers

amazon.com/author/sarasellers

bookbub.com/authors/sara-sellers

www.ingramcontent.com/pod-product-compliance
Lightning Source LLC
Chambersburg PA
CBHW031438200726
48289CB00002BA/660